TORMENT ME

A NOVELLA

THE ASHES BOYS

K.L. TAYLOR-LANE

ISBN eBook - 978-1-7392089-0-5
ISBN paperback - 978-1-7392089-1-2
Written by - K. L. Taylor-Lane
Cover design by – Leah Maree at Designs by LM.

❀ Created with Vellum

Remember, remember, the fifth of November,
Fireworks, Betrayal and Rot.

We have no desire,
To put out the fire,
She'll never escape from our plot.

Ashes Boys, Ashes Boys, she's locked in our sight,
And we'll tear down her King once we're done with
this night.

All that remains will be blood and bone,
Grimy old London we'll continue to own.

By The Ashes Boys she'll be caught dressed in red,
With malicious intent, a high price on her head.

Ashes Boys, Ashes Boys, let the flames rise,
Ashes Boys, Ashes Boys,
It's time for her demise.

For everyone who likes to be scared,
these psychos are for you.

A NOTE FROM THE AUTHOR

This is a why choose romance, in this story the female main character will have four love interests and will not have to choose.

Please be aware this novella contains **many** dark themes and subjects that may be uncomfortable/unsuitable for some readers. This novella contains **very** heavy themes throughout, so please heed the warning and go into this with your eyes wide open.

For more detailed information, please see pinned posts on the author's socials.

The characters in this story all deal with trauma

and problems differently, the resolutions and methods they use are not always traditional and therefore may not be for everyone.

This is a novella, meaning it is a **short** story, and it **does** end on a **cliffhanger**.

This book is written in British English. Therefore, some spellings, words, grammar and punctuation may be used differently to what you are used to. If you find anything you think is a genuine error, please do not report, instead, contact the author or one of her team to correct it. Thank you!

This book and its contents are entirely a work of fiction. Any resemblance or similarities to names, characters, organisations, places, events, incidents, or real people is entirely coincidental or used fictitiously.

CHAPTER 1
EMBER

The strong, familiar tang of copper floods my mouth, my teeth tearing into the delicate skin of my gnawed bottom lip, soothing me somewhat as my heart pounds inside my chest.

Blood.

The release it can bring. When things get to be just a little bit too much, and your skin gets all itchy and tight and you just wanna tear it the fuck off. Bare your insides to your outsides and slither out of it completely. The way the cool touch of a sharp edge pressing into pale skin, blood beading at the surface under the pressure, can feel like the only controllable release you'll ever fucking get.

Control is a fickle thing.

An illusion.

I have zero.

Sucking my lip into my mouth, I frown down at the fat red droplet hitting the carpet beside my foot, the very new, very *white* carpet. Fingers still plucking and pulling at the plastic-coated laces on my black boots. I stall my movements, worrying my lip with my teeth all over again at the very noticeable mark. It doesn't matter that this is *my* room, it's still my mother's house.

Huffing out a breath, I glance over my shoulder, eyes on the closed door, warm yellow light peeking beneath it from the hall. The music from downstairs drifting up, chatter and clinking glasses. I snuck up here to change, avoid more of the disappointed glances being tossed in my direction by my parent's snooty friends. I don't want to attend *this* Bonfire Night party, I want to go out and experience something real.

You'd think being twenty-two, I wouldn't need to sneak out. Especially not for something as innocent as a Bonfire Night party of all things. I can already hear fireworks shooting off in the distance, the soft echo of bangs and booms calling me to get closer. *Be burnt.* But here I am, worrying about being caught with the *wrong* shoes on after eight-pm.

The James family are all about appearances these days. Should be used to it now, I suppose. Ever since Dad got a big promotion at the hospital he worked at, some sort of top transplant surgeon award and a big fat cheque later, here we are, in Amberwood fucking Hills. Where, FYI, there are absolutely no fucking hills.

Mum went from juggling two jobs with two kids and a shift working husband she never got to see, to a glorified fucking housewife. And when I say housewife, I mean like one of those women on those fancy reality shows. Not a housewife that actually runs the house, I'm talking, dressing head to toe in designer clothes, has a separate set of pearls and diamonds for every day of the week. A *lady that lunches* and can't remember how to plug a hoover in, let alone run one over a carpet. I have nothing against women that enjoy that lifestyle, it's just… not supposed to be my mum.

Things have been different since all that, it's like they don't remember who we *really* are, where we come from, where they came from. The tightly packed, high rise tower blocks, flats sitting forty floors high, steel edged stairs and juddery lifts that didn't ever work. The old homeless guy that squatted on the seventh floor stairwell, looked fucking terrifying but was fiercely protective of us as kids when we were all playing outside.

It was raw and dirty and bleak. There were no opportunities, no jobs, the ones you could get, didn't cover even half the council estate rent. There was no future there that didn't involve gangs, running drugs or weapon dispensing. The people were rough, *we* were rough, we had holes in our jeans not created for fashion and bumming a cigarette off your next door neighbour, who was only a year older than you at the age of twelve, was all normal.

I miss it more and more every fucking day.

I think that's what I miss most about it.

The normality of it all.

Sometimes, I think it's all inside my head. That we've always lived here in our big house full of privilege, and I've fabricated my former life. Sometimes, I think my memories aren't really mine at all, burnt up, incinerated, stolen away like they're ash, drifting off in the gentlest of breezes, slipping through my fingers like smoke.

Cling on to them.

Replay them over and over inside my head.

Make myself remember.

I try to force a smile to my face, the memories

usually helping me breathe just a little easier, the tightness of anxiety in my chest, loosening for just a moment. Everything since we moved here has just been me taking it one day at a time, working out ways to get through each one better than the last. We've lived here ten years now and some days it's like trudging through four feet of sludge, thick mud that's slowly sucking me down, making everything just that little bit harder to do. To face.

I think, sometimes, that perhaps, I was just born sad.

And Danny, my older brother by seven years, just, *wasn't*. But then, he's also a boy, and I know boys were a big deal to my parents when they tried for their second but they got me instead. They were told right through the pregnancy the sex of their baby was a boy, and then I popped out, minus the equipment they were so desperately longing for. Maybe I was cursed right from conception. Pretty sure my mother feels that way. I know she loves me, in her own way. But I'm a burden, *'I'm not good with girls'* she'd always say, *'little boys are so much easier'*.

He got it easy right off the bat. Even before, when we weren't here. He was still always the child paraded around, which suited me just fine because I absolutely *never* wanted that. Except, I always wanted the comfort, the praise, the *attention* he was gifted so generously by my parents and grandparents alike. But maybe I only wanted it because I never knew what it was like to have it and *not* want it...

Anyway, Danny's perfect. Twenty-nine, an up and coming criminal defence lawyer, a know-it-all attitude to match and a constant, obnoxious running commentary on my very pitiful existence. We're such polar opposites, I don't think you'd even know we were related if we didn't look so alike.

We both have the curly blonde hair, mine a mess, hanging all the way down my back, his is always pulled out curls, styled back and over to one side. Matching bright blue eyes, mine ringed in sapphire, his just these endless depths of blue. And we both have slim builds, my five-foot-nine to his six-feet. When we're side by side, we are absolutely the James children.

A blessing and a curse. A blessing because I never have to attend the boring award ceremonies, conferences and trips away. And a curse because I am the child without success, a future, any chance at all at achieving something great. I'm just average, which is what I like, even if it hurts to see the disappointment in my parents' faces when I have nothing *remarkable* to tell them.

I work my job in the coffee shop in the town's high street, I wear black jeans, a black t-shirt and a purple apron. My hair shoved up into a thick pony-tail without a scrap of make up on my face. I talk to my customers like I'm their friend because some-times I'm the only social contact they have in a day, and people get lonely. *I* get lonely and I'm constantly surrounded by people living in this house. I don't need to go to law school or train as a doctor to make a difference. I already do. Just not in the way my parents would have liked, I guess. Prob-ably because my job of making hot drinks and toasting sandwiches won't win me any awards. But I'll never care about that, I just want to be seen for who I am and not what I'll never be.

I don't really think anybody understands that.

There was a boy once who did.

Or maybe he didn't.

But it felt like perhaps he could, and now my memories of him are just as much ashes to the wind as I am.

Grabbing an oversized black hoodie, I pull it over my head, covering my white long sleeve t-shirt tucked into black jeans. Sweeping my hair free from beneath the collar, leaving it down because it's so thick, hoping it'll help keep me warm whilst I'm standing outside for the fireworks.

Della, a girl I work with, who I guess is sort of my friend? I've never really had one before so it's sorta hard to tell, is picking me up on the corner outside of the community gates. Meaning all I have to do is get to her...

I unlock the French doors leading onto my balcony, I'm already at a slight advantage because I overlook the long curving driveway, and the guests my parents have over are all supposed to be in the back of the house. Guests, they want me out of sight of. So, if I play this right, I should be in the clear.

Pulling my hood up, tucking my hair inside, I step out onto the stone. Cold wind instantly whipping around me, I tug the doors closed at my back. Flattening myself against the side of the house, I watch Terry, one of the nicer security guards pass by below and with one final look left and right, I throw my legs over the carved stone railings and drop down.

The trellises bite at my hands, wisteria, its usual bright lavender colour gone with the summer, thick, rough vines left in its wake, I scale my way down.

The wind blows harshly, my body knocking into the stone wall beneath as I hurry my way down. my foot slips, a thin branch snapping beneath my boot and I imagine, for just a minute, what it would feel like to fall. Bones breaking, skin splitting, blood oozing, hot and thick as it spills over my skin, everything hidden in the shadows.

Shaking my head, I work a little faster, fumbling my way to the ground faster and faster. My boots hit the grass first, body dropping into a crouch, breath bursting free of my lungs with an oomph. I stay hidden behind a wall of thick bushes. Peering around it, eyes squinting in the dark, I place the flat of my hand over some orange berried branches, pushing down slightly to see better. I watch Terry make his way back, counting the twenty-six seconds it takes him to round the corner and then I bolt.

The thorny branches of the shrubbery snag my hands and sleeves as I throw myself out of their branches. Feet hammering heavily down the gradual decline of the brick driveway, I can see my breath, a foggy puff of white in the dark as I get to the front gates. Turning sideways, the guardhouse sitting empty as the person on duty no doubt does a perimeter check, I press up onto my tiptoes and shimmy through the gate when I hear Terry bellowing for me up by the house.

"EMBER JAMES!"

My heart rate spikes, adrenaline bolting through me like a rocket as I shove my way through the iron bars, my thick hoodie slowing me down, my face angled towards the road beyond, Terry's heavy footfalls rushing towards me. And just as I feel him snag my elbow, I pop free on the other side of the gates.

"Sorry, Terry!" I throw over my shoulder, ripping my sleeve free from his tight hold, the gates beginning to open at their usual slow pace as he shouts into his walkie-talkie.

But I don't hear anything he says, I'm off and running towards the waiting blue car I spy on the corner. Throwing open the back door of Della's car, my arse hitting the backseat, body flopping onto my side as I slam the door shut behind me.

"Go, go, go!" I yell, her foot slamming down on the accelerator, tyres skidding on the tarmac, we peel out of Amberwood Hills, racing towards the dark fields beyond.

CHAPTER 2
EMBER

Della chats my ear off as we head towards the farmland at the edge of town, I crawled into the front seat beside her when we finally got a safe distance away from the house. From what she tells me there's supposed to be an old farmhouse in the centre of corn fields. The thought alone makes me break out in goose-bumps. Horror movies always start with an abandoned house in the middle of nowhere, surrounded by fields of ridiculously tall crops, that way the serial killer can get you without you ever suspecting a thing. It sends a chill through me, my mind suppressing dark memories from pushing forward.

I'm being brave.

I take a deep breath, staring out of the passenger side window into the darkness. Only the bright flare of our headlights illuminating the winding country roads ahead of us. I tug the seat belt tighter, the bite of the thick material clawing into my hipbones, fingers curled around the belt across my chest.

As we drive, the pitch darkness the only thing surrounding us, my breathing hitches a little, my chest getting just the tiniest bit tight, I squeeze my eyes closed to think about anything but the dark. I don't think I really thought this through. An adventure, I'd thought, something different. Della talked about it all week, every shift we had together she practically begged me to come. Something about a guy from the *wrong* side of the tracks that she'd been having a wild love affair with... *inside her head*. Apparently, he doesn't even know her name but she's hoping if she turns up tonight, he'll be enthralled by her and fall at her feet, despite her being a *rich bitch*.

I'm more than a little sceptical but I'm not going to tell her that either.

I've never had a love affair, a boyfriend or, well, a relationship of any kind actually, so what do I know? But I'm almost positive that is not how it works. But Della's nice to me and kind of a friend, so I don't really think she'll appreciate me pointing out the flaws in her plan. Instead, I just nod my head, offer her the occasional -sort of- smile, and tell her I'll be behind her one hundred percent. Honestly, I'm just grateful I'm going to a party that isn't the usual stuffy formal affairs my parents hold and either force me to attend or lock me up in my bedroom, so no one accidentally stumbles across me.

"Sooo…" Della says lowly, breaking me free from my thoughts.

I glance to my right, her manicured hands gripping the steering wheel tightly. A thick, pale pink, cable knit jumper dress on her slim body, woollen, black tights beneath knee high black boots, all of it covered with a knee length puffer jacket in a light grey. She runs a hand through her long, highlighted hair, blue eyes flicking back to the empty road then back to me.

"How's it feel to be free, you little rebel?" she asks, her dark eyebrows dancing across her forehead.

"Um, I don't know yet," I laugh nervously, twisting my hands in my lap. "I'm kind of…" I trail off, unsure how to word what I want to say.

"Nervous." She nods. "I get it, but I'll be there with you, we can leave whenever you want, just let me know and we'll drive back," Della smiles, her pink lipstick bright against her white teeth.

"Okay," I whisper, swallowing the ball of anxiety in my throat.

I didn't think about being this far out from civilisation, if I call a cab, they're not going to trek all the way out here to rescue me. Goddamn, I should never have come, I didn't think this through, like, at all. I'm going to literally be stuck here, in the middle of nowhere, in the dark. Oh, Jesus Christ, what the hell am I-

"We're here!" Della squeals, my head snapping in her direction, wriggling in her seat, sitting up straighter, elbows bent, eyes wide, she leans forward, peering over the top of the steering wheel.

Following her gaze, the sky above endless rows of corn glowing a deep red, a huge bonfire licking at the moonlit sky. I shiver, staring up at it, eyes fixated on what looks like the mouth of a hell dimension, it's terrifying. I hear the music before the shack-like farmhouse comes into full view. Vehicles parked haphazardly all around, Della picks a place between two huge trucks, backing in and breaking too hard. I gasp as my seat belt tightens across my chest, the rumble of the engine dying out beneath us, I exhale, my shaky fingers finding and releasing the button.

Della jumps out, stripping off her thick winter coat, making me frown. She laughs as I step out of the car, about to pull on my leather gloves from the front pocket of my hoodie.

"Trust me, you do not want those on," thumbing over her shoulder in the direction of the house. "It's as hot as the seventh level of hell in there, leave the gloves, ditch the hoodie."

"Oh, I don't know, I mean, we're going to be outside, right? For the bonfire, fireworks?" cocking my head in question, I watch as she tries to tuck her smile into her cheek, the action making me border-line uncomfortable, but then she just shrugs.

"Sure," she says, "but you're better off leaving the hoodie in the car, we can always come and get it if you do get cold," pulling the V neckline of her jumper dress down further, the top of her bra cups on display, she looks up at me from beneath her lashes.

She fluffs her straight hair with her fingers, I find myself unconsciously pulling my black hoodie off and over my head, dropping it into the passenger seat and slamming the door shut. I stare down at it for a minute through the glass, suddenly feeling overly exposed in a tight white t-shirt. It has a round neck just grazing my collarbones and long sleeves that are a little too long. So I'm fully covered, but it's tight, tucked into my jeans, the material practically sculpted to my breasts and small waist. My fingers go to the door handle with the intention of retrieving my hoodie and pulling it back over my head, just as the car beeps signalling it's locked. Della steps around the car towards me. Swallowing hard, her arm looping through mine, seemingly not sensing my discomfort or stiffness at all, she half drags me towards the house.

I hate people touching me, even like this, casual, I have an aversion to it all. I just... I don't like it, it makes my skin itch, my muscles cramp, joints lock, everything inside of me screaming to break free. But I focus on how loose the hold is, how easily I could free myself, if I wanted. How Della's touch is just a little over friendly as opposed to something *else*.

Leftover pumpkins line the curving dirt pathway, their orange flesh dull and decaying where they've been left out in the elements. Muddy ground sticky with the fine fog rolling around our ankles. A sign for the *Haunted Corn Maze* sits crookedly upon two wooden stakes, a flickering solar light illuminating only half the jaggedly written words, set at one side of the pitch black entrance. My heart pounds in my chest, my breathing picking up, I blink quickly, finding my grip tightening on Della's arm, desperately trying to calm my fear, despite how foreign it feels to *want* to cling onto someone.

It's not Halloween anymore, you won't be going inside there, relax.

It makes my feet move a little quicker, though, desperation to get inside the house, rather than hide back in the car, alone, in the dark. Desperate now to find some light, I don't mind when Della's pace picks up too, a little quicker than mine. Although, I think hers is from excitement as opposed to fear. The noise from the farmhouse growing, a tinny, heavy bass booming, that along with a mixture of people's voices, crashes over me like a wave as someone opens the front door, the overwhelming sounds following them out. Which is when I notice there aren't many people hanging outside at all, but looking around, I see the bonfire seems to be at the back of the house, so maybe they're just more in that direction.

Three rickety steps lead up to the porch, which

we both take tentatively, our arms still linked, the wood once painted white, rotten and unstable beneath our boots. I don't touch the handrail, eyeing it, even in the dark, I can see the jagged splinters. Focusing on it just a touch too long, makes me think of the spiky wood poking beneath my skin. The bite of pain, sting of blood as it oozes from the wound. I snatch my wandering hand back just as quickly as I unconsciously reached out with it, locking my eyes ahead instead.

From the cold whistle of wind standing on the porch to the blazing inferno of heat that licks my skin like flames when we enter the farmhouse. It's such a stark contrast, sweat beads along my nape instantly, my mass of blonde curls only helping it gather there.

People are wall to wall, bodies moving and grinding all over one another. The air is heavy with sweat, thick with hormones, everything mixing with a cloud of smoke, cigarettes, something sweeter, the bonfire. It's sensory overload with the darkness, glow of the fairy lights around the ceiling, what appears to be an overhead light switched on in a room in the back of the house. Della pulls me inside, the door slamming closed behind us, she weaves us through the crowd of dancers, switching her hold on my arm, to take my hand in hers instead. Not enough space between bodies for me to even attempt to catch a full breath, as arms and chests brush against me, her grip firm over my knuckles.

My heart rate spikes wildly, breath hitching as I try desperately to make my way through them all without anyone touching me. Try and fail. By the time we reach the open space of the brightly lit kitchen, with tiles and flooring that looks to be from the nineteen-fifties, I'm just about ready to pass out. My face must be as red as the crimson lit sky above the bonfire, lungs desperately tight in my chest. Della releases my hand, managing to suck in a sharp breath, my body clawing for air, I catch my breath easier without her touching me. Focusing on staring out into the pitch darkness of the open back door.

The kitchen is clearer, less than a handful of people, counters full of drinks, beer, spirits, mixers, blue and red plastic cups, a punch bowl full of something dark pink.

Brushing my clammy palms down my thighs, the soft denim of my jeans still a little cool from the outside air, I peer around the space. Nobody paying me much attention, bar a quick glance from the woman across the other side of the kitchen. I shuffle my back to the nearest wall, no one able to sneak up on me, my eyes able to view the entire room. Della picks her way through the different bottles on the countertop, twisting lids, and pouring mixtures, popping back up in front of me with two blue cups filled with some rancid smelling concoction.

Standing before me, her body angled in just such a way, she can still easily see into the front room. Bringing her drink to her lips, eyes over the rim of the cup, they widen, almost comically, and then she's spluttering down her drink, half choking, before slamming the cup into my free hand so hard it makes my wrist crack. Liquid sploshing over its sides, running down and over my hand, sticky in the webbing between my fingers.

"Shit! He's here. How do I look?" she hisses the question at me, eyes still locked on the front room over my shoulder.

Too close to my face, my body automatically shrinking back into the wall. Della doesn't seem to notice, pressing her body almost flush with mine as she bares her teeth in my face.

"Am I good?"

I nod in response, her white teeth free of lipstick and anything else she thinks might be there. My heart hammering hard in my chest, grip on the two cups too tight, the thick plastic crinkling beneath my fingers, and just when I think I'm about to pass out from holding my breath, Della steps back. Relief rushes through me, a nervous chuckle on the tip of my tongue, she runs her fingers through her hair, tossing the length over her shoulder.

"You good?" she asks then, her blue eyes flicking to mine, a singular raised brow on her forehead.

"Oh, I, um…"

She looks to me again, dragging her eyes between me and the guy she's stalking. Nodding, closing my gaping mouth before I catch flies. She snatches her drink back, downs it in one, returning the empty cup to my seemingly waiting hand and bounces off into the crowd at my back.

I stand still for a moment, a hard blink clearing my hazy vision, shaking off my shock, I glance up, take in the now empty room around me. I didn't think she'd actually leave me… like, alone, and at least not this quickly. I don't really know what I thought. Probably didn't think any of this excursion through properly at all.

That bite of anxiety spikes again, the tiny hairs along my arms rising, a prickling at the nape of my neck. I shuffle forward, placing both cups, mine still full, down onto the counter. Hands splaying on the cracked marble top, a heavy sigh releases itself before I can stop it. My eyes squeezing closed for *just* a second.

"You look lost, pretty girl."

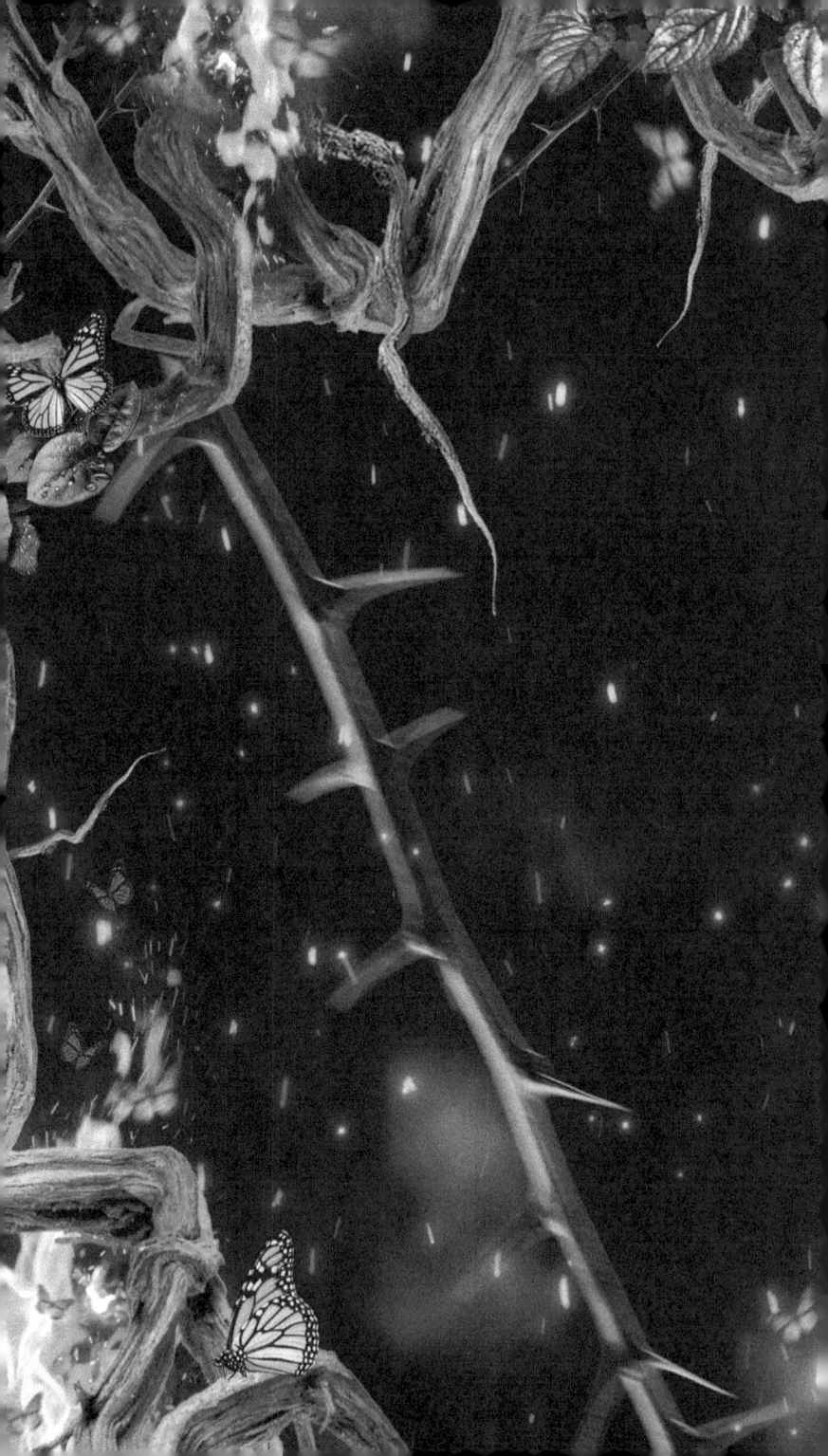

CHAPTER 3
BLAZE

I stand with my back to the corner, foot kicked up beside the rear entrance in the brightly lit kitchen. Cracked lino, scuffed surfaces, creaky cabinets with unsteady hinges on their doors. A sink with taps that splutter, cracked windows and rotten spots in the flooring, and that's just the down-stairs. The wooden staircase that takes you up, well, upstairs is off limits, for a multitude of reasons, not that anyone could safely make it up there anyway, perhaps if they had luck on their side, but it seems unlikely with the problematic wood steps. No one would get far but the four of us.

Surveying the masses, the kitchen empty at my presence, the way I like it to be, I run my sharp gaze over the crowd of dancing bodies. The air thick, with sex and smoke, the cold November wind blowing in fiercely through the open door beside me, but nothing could cool down the temperature in here. Not with this amount of people crowded inside.

Bonfire Night is the one night a year I allow my boys to really let loose, all of their demons free to come out and play. Flint with his psychotic grin and childlike excitement for setting shit on fire. Cole and his cold, deadly calm, luring his victims in with his gently coaxing voice and deceptive charm. Phoenix's cool indifference, obsession with forced smiles, and suppressed kink for flames. I let them have free reign on Guy Fawkes, anything goes, and then I clean up the mess. Always in control, even when they're not, *especially* when they're not.

My dark eyes flare over the open space of the house, people coming and going, looping away from the open kitchen when they see me hovering inside. No one I observe is piquing my interest. I'm eternally bored. Everything in this life is boring, I need a chase, seek a thrill, feel the fight. I want tears and passion. A dying inferno just barely swirls around inside me, spitting nothing but embers and ash, forever waiting for an accelerant to relight the blaze.

My fingers tighten around the neck of my beer bottle, bringing it to my lips, knuckles cracking around the glass. Cocking my head, I watch Della Patrick waltz inside, head held high, shoulders back. She always turns up here acting like she owns the place. Every time we throw a party, desperation for a little slice of bad boy, wafts off of her like her overpriced, dishwater perfume. Me and my boys wouldn't touch her with a fucking bargepole, and anyway, I'm certainly not looking to get some rich bitch all up on my dick. Too needy, too whiney, entitled, all of them the fucking same.

I want someone I can dominate, but I want someone that's not going to fucking whinge about it afterwards. They all say they want to be choked out until you actually thread your fingers around their skinny little necks and squeeze. Then they're bitching about bruises on their fucking trachea and how I'm such a monster. As if that's a fucking insult. I want to cut off their air, I *need* to be the only thing they straddle between life and death. I am the knife's edge, sharp, precise, murderous.

I say if they live.

I say if they die.

What.

When.

How.

Crying, fighting, screaming, all of those things are a necessity at this point, giving me just enough to hold my attention while I'm battering their cervix. I don't know what the fuck it'd take to actually *keep* my wavering attention. I don't sleep around, I could be faithful, I'm loyal to a fucking fault at this point, but no one is worthy.

For me.

For us.

The Ashes.

Gritting my teeth, I gulp down the rest of my beer, slamming the empty green bottle down onto the counter just a little too hard, a tremor from the force pulsing up my forearm. My dark eyes narrow in on Della, her effortless weave through the writhing bodies in the front room, practised, because she's been here *way* too many fucking times. She's heading my way, and I still don't think she understands what everyone else here does.

When I'm in the room, you're just... *not*.

I could stand here, assert my dominance, bend her into submission, humiliate, make her beg, cry. Sighing heavily, I start to retreat out of the back door and into the darkness instead.

She's not even worth the meagre effort.

It would be too easy.

Boring.

And I am so, so bored.

My feet take me back another step, the open door at my back, I slip through. Della twines through the last dancers as the darkness swallows me up. Keeping me tucked just out of view in my outfit of all black, when a second person is popping into the empty space with her.

Bright blonde curls are what draw me in, a thick fucking mess of them tangled over her slim shoulders, light coloured ringlets spun all the way down to her tight waist. A crimson ribbon through the front, looped at the nape of her neck, tied on top in a bow. My fingers curl into tight fists at my sides, the image inside my head of split, bloodied knuckles twisting up in her lengths, crimson smearing across her milky, pale cheek. White long sleeve t-shirt sculpted to her tits, my eyes trace down her body, following the dip of her navel, the high waistband of her skinny black jeans curved tightly over her hips, clinging to her thighs. Black boots, laces loose, but it doesn't look purposeful, more like they slipped undone, and she just hasn't noticed yet, halfway up her thin calves.

I tilt my head, predatory instincts broiling in my

veins. Something spiking beneath my skin, razor sharp and scalding hot. My heart starts to thud, hard and heavy in my chest, heat licking across my lower abdominal muscles. I feel myself shift in place, the icy cold wind of November doing nothing to chill my searing skin. My shoulders flex, muscles tensing beneath my rapidly tightening skin.

And then she looks up, backing herself into the yellowed wallpaper, Della stepping away, leaving her there. I watch her flush cheeks lose a little of their colour, the climbing red streaks up her throat dying down the more she forcefully slows her breathing. Her chest rises and falls too quickly, tits heaving. I home in on her throat, her pulse thrumming like the wings of a butterfly desperate to tear right through the skin.

Enthralled.

That's what I am in this moment.

Because when her sky blue eyes, bright and ringed with sapphire, flick over her surroundings, gliding over me hidden in the darkness beyond, I see her.

All wide doe eyes and plump pout, high cheekbones, thick lashes. A gentle smattering of pale freckles just over the bridge of her nose, a delicate scar beneath the outer corner of her left eye. A scar

I'm intimately familiar with because *I* gave it to her over ten years ago. I'm not sure what it is I'm feeling in the moment, so many rioting thoughts rushing through my head. The prospect. Possibility. The plan.

All of the things I've been mulling over inside my head as The Ashes leader for so, so long. Biding my time.

Ensuring I don't make a rash decision.

Patiently waiting for the perfect opportunity to reveal itself.

And I think it just did…

I'm not sure I believe in fate, but if I did, I'd call this exactly that.

My cock thickens, irritably so, hardening to the point of pain beneath my tight black joggers, begging for a release it's not going to get. *Yet.* I bite down hard on my bottom lip, swallowing copper as I tear into the flesh, nostrils flaring, I watch Della move back in front of her friend.

I watch their interaction. Della unsurprisingly oblivious to the fact that Danny James's little sister looks overly fucking terrified to be here. There's a tremor in her fingers, grip tightening on her cup of fuck knows what, the way she inhaled the smell of it when it was handed to her though tells me that one, she is not a regular drinker, and two, she'll be a fucking lightweight. Both things I *could* use to my advantage tonight, but I won't. I don't need to, I'm more than capable of getting her under control.

She'll be under me and purring like a fucking kitten in no time.

God, I hope this kitty's got claws.

Della ditches her friend then, making the start to my plan of getting Ember alone, now completely null and void. My eyes flicker over her head momentarily, watching Liam Smith enter the house, Della practically running to get to him. I almost scoff, lips twisting up on one side. Good fucking luck to her if she wants to be tangled in that sticky web.

My skin itches hot, my fingers flexing at my sides, I want to pounce on her, scare the already frightened little rabbit even more. But I've gotta play this right if I want to pull it off well.

My head twists on my neck, watching her exhale a short sharp breath through her teeth, her chest falling, shoulders hunching forward. She stares down at the two cups in her hands, a crease pinching between her ashy brows. She steps forward, eyes lowered, placing them down on the countertop, I expect her to straighten, square her shoulders, reveal just a little of the sass I remember being on the other end of when she was a kid. But she just… doesn't.

Her eyes fasten shut, hands splaying over the counter, a defeated sigh rushing through her lips. She drops her head forward, limp between her tense shoulders.

I watch for a second, not understanding what I'm looking at, but my feet move me forward, out of the darkness into the bright yellow light of the kitchen. The cold air at my back dissolving with the heat from the front room flowing into the kitchen. I glare at the woman in the corner grabbing a drink, and she hightails it out of the kitchen like a frightened mouse.

She doesn't notice me, doesn't look up, guard down, leaving herself stupidly vulnerable. I lick my lips, watching her fingertips dig into the cracked counter, flexing until her nail beds are blanched white.

I stop, a mere foot away from her, she should sense me, at least feel the coolness of outside wafting off of my clothing as it slowly dies off, but it's like she's somewhere else. Lost inside her own head, thoughts all blurring into one. I wish I could see inside. Crack open her skull, peel back her scalp, the way I want to remove her clothes, peer inside her head, watch the way she works, dissect what makes her tick.

She still doesn't see me, it's been seconds, rushing by too fast for me, too slow for her. If I were a predator wanting to end her... *Well,* if I were a predator wanting to end her *now,* she'd be fucked. Her unawareness of what creature crept out of the dark, oblivious to the fact I'm cataloguing her every single twitch.

I almost like it... her ignorance.

A feeling of something like excitement pounds in my temples, my eyes practically bulging out of my head. Desperation to have her riding me hard enough to break me. And we can't have that before I've had the chance to break her...

"You look lost, pretty girl."

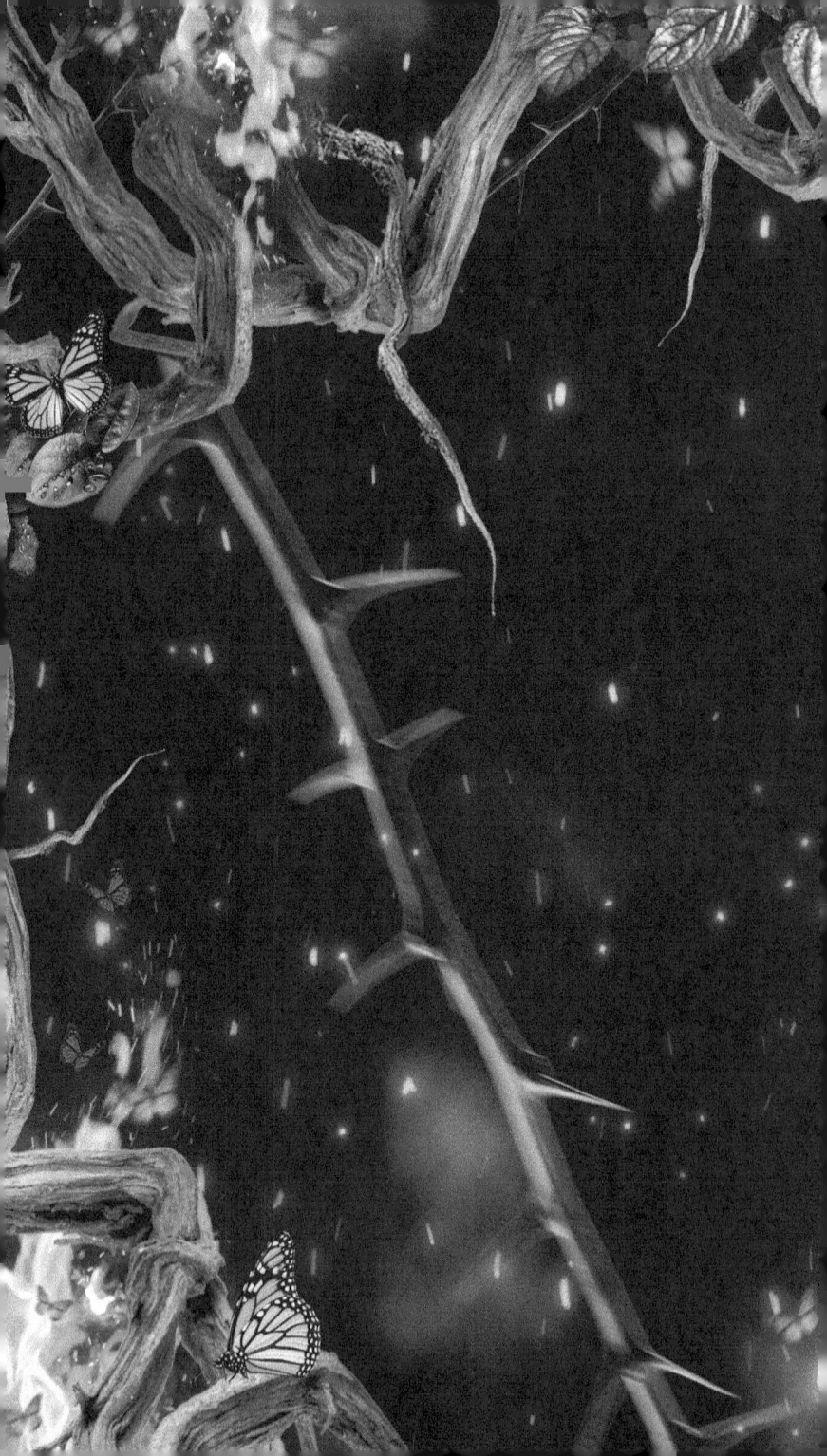

CHAPTER 4

EMBER

My eyes snap open, the deep husk of a voice rumbling through my bones. My hands ping up from the counter, balling at my chest, feet taking me a solid step back, instinct to run screaming through me. I let my guard down, I wasn't paying attention to my surroundings.

Stupid.

What the hell am I doing here?

I stumble back on my feet, a big hand, catching my elbow in a firm grip to steady me. I tear myself away on instinct, his touch singeing me through my thin sleeve. I bump back against the wall, my head smacking hard, arms up tight in front of my body, elbows tucked, I heave a breath. And then the flaring heat of embarrassment hits my cheeks. I don't dare look up at him. The stranger still stood beside the counter, I stare down at my feet, the peach coloured lino separating the toes of my boots and the toes of his black trainers.

My teeth grind unconsciously, a new wave of terror making me clench my jaw, waiting to be called a freak. I'm not good at being out, I never should have left the house, that much is clearer to me now in the last thirty seconds than it was in the entire thirty-minute drive over here. I'm actually surprised Terry and his team haven't come after me yet. I know there's a tracker in my phone, so it's only a matter of time.

I hold my breath, keep my hands balled at my chest, chin dipped so low it almost brushes my curled knuckles. My skin feels charred, like I've been thrown upon the pyre, flames scorching my skin into nothing but burnt, cracked debris. Oh, how I wish in this moment that that were true.

I watch with my breath held, my lungs on fire, the toes of his trainers becoming the whole of his trainers as he moves in closer. Tight cuffs around his ankles of his black joggers, tight on his muscular thighs. Olive skin stretched over large hands, hanging by his sides, green veins sharp and thick beneath. Jagged, criss-cross scars littering his knuckles, lines of black tattoo ink trailing down the back of his hands, the full designs hidden beneath the long sleeves of his black hoodie.

It makes me think of my own black hoodie, balled up and discarded in the empty car. How I wish, even more now, that I'd kept it on. I feel exposed.

I pull my bottom lip into my mouth, biting down until I taste iron in the back of my throat and have to swallow it away. It makes me draw in a sharp breath, my entire body starting to tremble. I know the back door is open, every now and then I can feel just the gentlest breeze of cool air twisting around my legs. If I just push forward, mumble out an apology, maybe shoulder him out the way if I absolutely have to, I don't like touch, and he's much bigger than me, the same way they were and I'm no-

"What are you thinking about, pretty girl?" he asks me, interrupting my erratic thoughts and in all my plotting to escape, I failed to realise he'd gotten closer again.

His warm minty breath from his words blows a stray curl forward of my hair bow, the long blonde ringlet catching in my lashes. I flinch back, inhaling sharply, the wall at my back, my spine bumps it a second time. Pain blooms at the back of my eyes and I squeeze them shut tight for just a moment. I catch his scent as I draw in a shuddery breath, caramel, smoke and spice. Strong, soft, dark, a statement. It smells like the night's air on Guy Fawkes. So, perhaps it's just our evening's surroundings that have affected him, maybe he always smells this way, possibly it's just his aftershave.

Or maybe he always smells like danger.

"Why don't we go outside and get you some fresh air?" the stranger asks me this time, my breathing raspy and shallow, a panic attack teetering just at the edges of my blurry vision.

His offer seems sincere, but my skin prickles at the back of my neck, something in the back of my mind whispering, *don't trust him.*

One of those big hands comes up in the small space between us, the green veins dark as moss up close, snaking like vines beneath his skin. My lashes flutter, nostrils flaring, I pull in a slow breath, like my brain just finally decided to reboot, kickstart itself and try to process what the hell is happening. The palms of my hands itch, my fingers still curling into them tightly, nails carving into the clammy skin where I hold them up tight at my chest.

"I don't bite," he chuckles, raspy and thick, seductively chaotic.

He's lying, my psyche whispers, *go back to the car, get your phone, call Terry.*

The process of thoughts smoulders, my heart seizing in my chest. All of the logical things I should do, could do. Find Della, get your phone, call Terry. They repeat over and over in my brain, time inside my head all but stands still, everything slow, too slow.

My arms drop at the same time my head does, chin crashing into my chest, eyes seeing nothing but black. I feel my body rush cold, muscles and bones liquefying, joints loosening until my knees shake. I expect, even in my half unconscious state that I'm going down, probably drop to my knees, hard against the floor, slide down the wall at my back, thunk to my bum. Instead, I feel heat, firm and kindling against my spine, warmth splintering out over my skin in a flurry.

"Come on, pretty girl, open your eyes," the order isn't snapped, it's purred, warm, cosy fire with a soft bite of playfulness, something that feels almost familiar.

I flinch at the sudden cold then, my eyes fluttering open as the heat at my back dies off, replaced with the cold plastic of a chair. The cold November air incinerating the foreign feeling I had with his overly gentle touch. Lifting my head up too fast, the top of my spine cracking as I do, a sharp crick in my neck, I spin my head on my shoulders, a jarring motion, making my teeth ache. Everything inside of me telling me not to lock eyes with this stranger.

Except, it's not *everything*. A teeny, tiny fragment inside my head, the depraved part inside of me that somehow still *enjoys* the fear, a part of me I'm petrified to admit exists in me at all, whispers, *look at him.*

I'm bound by the voice, an echo of fright vibrating in the compulsion.

I look up.

Dark brown hair, thick with loose curls, sits in a flop on top of his head, a singular curl fallen forward, just brushing the top of his rich eyebrow. High cheekbones, a wide square jaw, light peppering of dark stubble brushing his cheeks. A straight, strong nose, leading to full, dark blush lips, black hoop snagged through the left side of the bottom one. I track my gaze higher, settling on his dark eyes with a flinch. Rich, ebony brown, almost black in the absence of light, as pitch as the night's sky above us.

My breath held again, I tear my eyes from his,

fixate on a tiny scar, glistening under the pale moonlight, on the tip of his chin instead. His stare is blistering against my skin, I feel an unfamiliar heat lick at my insides, blazing butterflies soaring in my belly, combusting when the heat just becomes too much, incinerating their wings. My body much lower than his, being seated in a rickety garden chair, the warped plastic seat like ice in comparison to the heat rolling off of my body. Embarrassment, adrenaline, that feeling of just waking up, but still in a dreamlike state, all of it mixing inside my brain. Overwhelming, dangerous, something like longing for the unknown bristling through my veins.

"Look at me," another demand.

One snapping me back to the present, hearing returning in a thump, heavy bass from the house, crackling and spitting from the bonfire just a short distance away from the porch we're on. My knees lock, but everything else is drawn in, my eyes snap back unto his, and I see the flames dancing there. *Danger,* they scream, but that's the only sound I don't hear.

He wears a half smile, it's a tense curl of his lip that is probably more accurately a suppressed snarl, but it seems more genuine than not. A crease set between his dark eyebrows, he flares his nostrils, making me realise I've been staring silently for way too long. I drop my gaze, fingers knotting in my lap, pins and needles in my noodle-like arms. I swallow, licking my lips, desperate to get some sort of words out of my mouth, but nothing really feels appropriate.

I want to go home.

He's still staring at me, watching, waiting, and it feels oddly familiar, like he's watched me before, even though I have no idea where or how because I never leave my house. And then he's dropping down before me. A seamless movement, his large body folding gracefully into a hunched crouch, a little way away but still too close. I blink, staring at my hands balled on top of my thighs, as his large hand moves between us once more, slow, paced, visible to me, because he knows I'm spooked. Heat flushes in my cheeks, embarrassment possibly one of the worst emotions I've ever felt, I pray for the ground to swallow me up, bury me in its shadows until I can learn to forget this ever happened.

His thumb and finger take my chin, a gentle bite in the grip, enough to garner my body's natural response, a flinch, shockingly hard as it jolts through me, but he holds firm. No room for me to escape his grasp. He tilts my chin, subtly forcing me to meet his dark eyes. Something shifts in my brain as I look into them, and I feel a gentle frown develop between my brows.

"There you are," he hums, his tongue darting out, rolling over his bottom lip, his teeth tug on his lip ring, eyes never leaving mine. "What are you so afraid of, pretty girl?"

Oh, what a question.

Unable to form words, I, too, lick my lips. Desperate to form some kind of statement to burst free, but nothing happens, my brain dies. I let my gaze drop, despite my face angled up towards his.

"Uh-uh," he tuts, "look at me." I do, finally taking a much needed breath, his eyes flicking between my own.

"Sorry," I stutter then, a breathy whisper, something that feels automatic, more for my own discomfort than his, *unnecessary*.

"For?" he cocks his head, a smirk on those thick lips now, taunting, a thrum along the back of his jaw.

"I- um… for what happened, I'm not very good-"

"With crowds," he says.

At the same time, I say, "with people."

I cringe, his smirk turning into a wicked grin,

one that's gone as fast as it appeared, making me wonder if I even saw it at all. His hold on my chin pinching tighter, I don't move, something changing in the air between us. Suddenly feeling like I'm in the presence of a predator, it's probably advisable to hold still, is it not? Isn't that what they tell you to do in the wild when faced with a lion or a bear?

He nods then, licking across his front teeth, he releases his hold on me, standing to his full height, towering over me at something like six-foot-four, a giant of a man in comparison to my five-nine. Hand out, palm up, he raises a brow on his head in question, eyes tracking me. I stand on my own, scooting just a little to the right, away from his hand, my back to the bonfire beyond. It's a contrast of ice and heat, his body temperature seeming to burn up the cold air between us, the fire at my back, the cold night's air. Goosebumps prickle across my flesh, confusion in whether I'm cold or warm, I shiver. A movement he catches with dark eyes that appear to be seeing everything.

"Let's get a drink."

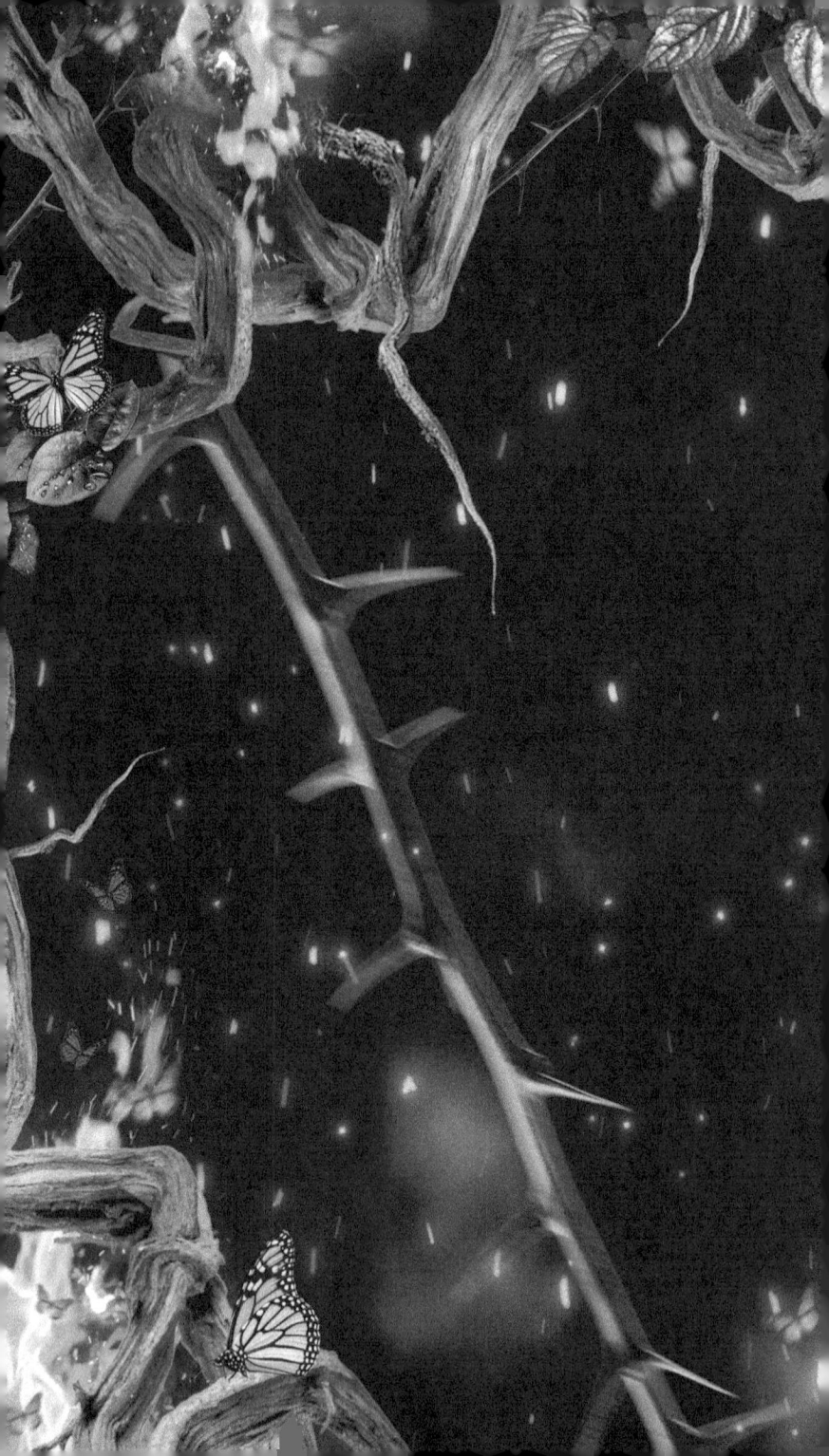

CHAPTER 5
COLE

Blaze stands, offering the blonde girl his hand, smooth bastard, turning on the charm. I don't know where he found her because I certainly didn't see her come in. She looks like some prissy bitch playing a damsel in distress. I dunno what he's trying it on with her for, she's not gunna let him choke her out while she's struggling on the end of his dick.

I scoff, turning my attention elsewhere, the huge pyre before me, roaring with flames, the base of the bonfire a heavy blue, sparks and embers spitting from the top. Wood peeling and cracking in its centre, the hiss and sizzle of fire, echoing laughter from the darkened fields surrounding. Couples and groups braving the pitch dark corn fields, finding themselves a secluded place to fuck.

I scrub a hand over my short hair, tight black afro curls, not quite long enough to actually be curly. The sides and back shaved in a fade, short beard trimmed and neat on my face. I twist one of my black stud earrings, a small flat disc in each ear, I twiddle it between my finger and thumb, around and around. Staring at the flames, it does something to my insides, twisting my core with a thumping heat, my cock stirring in my tight joggers.

Arousal.

From fire, heat, flames.

Pyrophilia.

An unusual kink, it would seem, for someone who's body is forty percent covered in burn scars. But I thrive with the control, the fire and flames lick at skin in the way *I* decide. I control the flammable substances, the amount, the time, the place, the where and the when. It's all up to me. That delicate balance between warming skin and burning it, when to put out the flames, when to let them burn a little longer.

My eyes locked on the roaring fire before me, slowly zoning out as I stare at its blue core, feeling the heat from the flames lick my skin, like the forked tongue of the devil is tasting me. Wondering how long it'll be before he can feast on my burnt soul. I smile softly at that, thinking of my end.

The amount of near misses I've had; I'm probably going to live forever at this rate. Or, I guess, at least until my luck runs out. Gang life is a hard one, there are no fluffy bedtime stories, romantic tales of love, promises of safety and eternal life. Just grime and shit and flames.

"What ya doin'?"

My eyes narrow on instinct, Flint's lilt in my ear, breath down my neck. Slinking out of the shadows, like some sort of psychotic, horror movie, serial killer. All of which is accurate. But our version, The Ashes version, is a little happier than classic horror villains. He's too happy and lively for my liking. Still, at least one of the four of us has a believable smile, even if it is a little crazed.

"Nothing," I grunt, my deep voice low.

"Did you see her?" Flint questions, his body shifting to stand beside mine, pale skin glowing orange in the light of the red flames.

"Who?" I ask, already knowing, because Flint always does tend to fixate on the women Blaze picks out.

I think he just likes giving his adopted, older

brother a bit of healthy competition if I'm honest. Both men have a charm they can turn on to the point of sickening. I don't have charm. Phoenix has even less. It's why he has to make all of his victims smile after, cause he sure as shit couldn't get them to do it before.

"The girl, all that thick hair," I see him lick his lips out the corner of my eye, his gaze locked on the fire before us. "She's so nervous," he says with awe, his hand going down to adjust his dick in his jeans. "I bet her fear tastes like syrup."

"Flint."

"I bet she likes to be burnt," he sighs whimsically, making me snap my head in his direction.

"Flint," I'm colder this time, lower, a slight bite in my tone.

The man and his obsessions never, ever end well, and I do not want him enticing me into his madness by using the prospect of fire to lure me in. Flint is a pyromaniac; he's compelled to set shit on fire without any reason or rhyme other than the fact he itches until he does it. Pyromania and pyrophilia are two completely separate things. We're both sated and satisfied by fire in different ways.

I watch his side profile, his eyes still firmly

locked on the fire, but he knows I'm staring at him, his lips curve, just enough to be called a smile.

"I don't want to hurt her," slowly rolling his eyes onto mine, a small crease at the outer corner of his right one, still facing the bonfire, the flames turning his glacial blue orbs into orange tinted infernos. "I want to play with her."

"Flint."

"Stop saying my name like that," he hisses, finally turning his face to mine.

He's taller than me, all of us, younger than Blaze and I, older than Phoenix, but sometimes he has the mind of a child. Obsessive impulses that are hard to curb, needs and wants that cannot be fulfilled in a traditional way. He takes and hides and cherishes, until he just loses interest and forgets all about the bodies and damage he leaves behind.

"I'm going to find Nix," he tells me then, that happy lilt back in his deep voice, an air of amusement on his tongue. "He might let me fuck him while I wait for Blaze to be done with his little doll."

Flint turns to leave, hands pushing back his black hair, pocketing them on his way back towards the fields.

"Flint," I call, gruff but soft, I don't ever have to raise my voice to get the attention I demand.

"Yes?" he asks sweetly, looking back at me over his broad shoulder.

"Wait for Blaze to tell you it's your turn."

His lips twist to one side, his smile falling, knowing I'm right, he nods stiffly before turning away and disappearing into the dark crops.

CHAPTER 6

EMBER

S tanding in the kitchen, the stranger's back
to me, the room once again emptying as we
entered, at his presence over mine. I study
his lean shape from behind, a swimmers body with
packed planes of muscle, the sleeves of his black
hoodie tight, clinging to him like a second skin. His
skinny fit jogging bottoms doing the same thing,
tight over the solid curve of his arse, snug on his
muscular thighs. I watch from my place in the
corner of the kitchen, humming refrigerator to my
right, the corner where the counters meet kissing
the centre of my spine.

The dark eyed man turns back to face me, an
orange plastic cup in either hand. I cock my head
just slightly, taking in his face again, something too

familiar about it but I can't place what. Something in my brain that I can't quite seem to latch onto. And then he's hovering before me, close enough to block me in, but far enough away that I could ram my way to the exit if I really needed to. I already feel like I don't really *want* to.

"Drink," he says, deep and smooth, a filled orange cup held out in offering.

I eye it warily for a moment, then the cup's moving from my field of vision. He takes it to his lips, tipping it back, swallowing down a large mouthful, Adam's apple bobbing in his throat, before offering it up to me again. My gaze flicks to the drink, up to his dark eyes.

"It's not spiked," he shrugs, my eyes dropping back to the drink in question.

Raising my hand, I take the cup, my fingers brushing his much larger ones, I snatch it from his grip. Stare down into the dark coloured mixture, will the heat in my cheeks to disappear, the squirmy feeling beneath my skin to dissolve.

"Sip it, Emmy, I wouldn't drug you."

My head whips up so fast, I slosh the drink over its sides, soaking my hand and the floor in the process. My eyes snapping to his, recognition hitting me like a punch to the gut, my lungs seize, heart thudding hard.

"Blaze?" I question in disbelief, my lips popping open in surprise.

The older boy that lived in my old block of flats, friends, sort of, with my brother, once upon a time. He used to walk me to school sometimes, when my mum was working, Dad was at the hospital, Danny had left me home alone. My free hand reaches up of its own accord, finger brushing over the tiny scar beneath my left eye. He smiles then, his hand coming to mine. I drop it before he makes contact, but the pad of his thumb doesn't stop on its way to my face. He brushes his calloused skin over the silky scar, my eyes flutter closed and I suddenly feel tears prick the backs of my eyes.

Everything I remember *is* real.

Sometimes when I'm lonely, I think of the tall boy with the bronze skin and dark eyes. His kind smiles and protection. We lived in a rougher area, not safe for little girls to walk to and from school alone. I think I probably had a little crush on him if I'm honest.

"You do remember," he says so softly I almost don't hear him, words uttered more to himself than to me.

Opening my eyes, surveying his gaze on his thumb, sweeping beneath my eye, the touch not making me shrink away, but filling my veins with an unfamiliar heat. My skin prickles at his touch, warmth filling my cheeks, I find myself leaning into it before he pulls away.

"Let's go upstairs, it's quieter and there're too many people down here. I want to catch up."

He looks right at me, eyes flicking between my own, my insides knotting and loose all at the same time. At the tilt of his head, I find myself agreeing with a slow nod, his large body instantly stepping back, giving me space to push off of the counter. He turns away from me then, and I pause, watching him take a couple steps towards the front room. Then he's looking over his shoulder, pausing his steps, a frown on his face, he stretches out his free hand, the one not clasping a drink. I eye it cautiously, unsure of taking it, but strangely wanting to, an internal battle taking place inside my brain.

I shuffle the short distance between us, tenderly taking his outstretched hand with my free one, the cup filled with the alcohol I won't be drinking, in the other. His thick fingers effortlessly curl around mine, a strong solid grip that I'm not sure I could break free from, should I want to. I follow his lead, the dancing crowd parting for him like the red sea. Everyone growing just a little quieter in a rolling wave of sound as they move aside.

Reaching the bottom of the stairs, Blaze turns to peer down at me over his shoulder. Heat in his stare as he quickly runs his eyes over me.

"The steps are rotten, follow where I put my feet, or you'll go through them."

"Okay," I whisper in response, suddenly regretting the decision to leave the areas filled with people.

He feels the tension in my hand at my hesitation, one of his feet already on the first stair. I swallow hard, dropping my gaze back to my feet, feeling the heat of the crowd at my back. I want to flinch away, away from them, but that would force me closer to Blaze and that's where my hesitation lies. I gnaw on my lip, worrying it between my teeth, my skin feels so hot, I want to claw it off. Slice it open, squeeze the wound, let it ooze and bleed, feel that mind numbing relief of a cut.

"Ember?"

I look up, Blaze's brown eyes fiery and harsh, I blink and it's gone, the danger dissolved as though it were never there to begin with.

"We can stay down here if you want, I just thought you might feel more comfortable upstairs." He shrugs casually, like he couldn't really care less either way but I'm not so sure that part's true at all.

"Do you own this place?" I ask then, suddenly unsure how I feel about being upstairs in a strangers house.

He cocks his head, a small smile of amusement on his face, "yes."

It's that simple.

Do I believe him?

Should I not?

Why shouldn't I?

Deciding to swallow my fear, I move closer, his grip on my hand tightening once again, like he loosened it, preparing himself for me to make my escape.

Or just let me think I could.

I follow each step he takes, each stair having us place our feet in slightly different positions. They creak and groan under his weight more than mine, making me feel just a little bit safer that I won't fall to my death, well, at least not before he will. The landing is in darkness when we reach the top. A dim glow of orange flickering in from the single window at the end of the long narrow hall.

It's an odd shape, this floor, a singular hallway with doors all along one side, each one pulled closed. Blaze leads me along in the dark, the floor feeling a little sturdier beneath my boots as he takes more confident steps than before. He leads us to the very far end of the hall, taking his time, passing six doors on the way to get there. He turns to look at me, releasing my hand, he twists the round, metal doorknob, pushing the door open. Stepping aside, hand holding his drink, arm outstretched into the dark room, gesturing me inside. I swallow, taking small tentative steps into the room.

The darkness feels too harsh, like my eyes could never work properly in here. The door at my back bangs shut and I jump, spinning to face Blaze, cocking his head at me. My heart thuds hard in my chest, liquid fire rolling through my veins, screaming its way through my tense body.

Blaze passes by me, moving around where I stand, I follow with my eyes, the general direction of where it feels like he's heading in the dark. Metal on metal screeches slightly, short curtains parted quickly, their metal rings clattering along the pole, light from the huge bonfire flooding into the room. Shoulders deflating, I pull in a slow shuddery breath, my body instantly relaxing at having some light in the room.

Blaze turns away from the window, flopping down onto the end of a small double bed. The mattress springs creak beneath his weight, pale coloured sheets dressing it. It all looks surprisingly well kempt for a run-down old house, the sheets look clean and the bed's made neatly. He pats his large hand over the space beside him, half of his face lit from the flames, the other half swallowed by shadows. I move in closer, slowly sinking down onto the bed beside him, more than a foot of space between us, but I can still feel the heat of him, his smoky caramel scent filling my nose.

The distance feels too close and too far, but I stay in place, one hand tight around my plastic cup, the other squeezing my knee so hard it makes my teeth grit. There's a silence between us, but I don't feel uncomfortable, I don't feel *comfortable*, but I'm somewhere in between and I decide that's good enough for now. I'm not exactly someone that ever really feels comfort.

I know Blaze.

Knew him.

Blaze is safe.

He protected me that day in the stairwell.

"How have you been?" he asks me, and I realise how right he was about being able to hear better up here.

The music from downstairs is just a lowly vibration pulsing through the soles of my shoes now. My chin still dipped, I look up at him through my lashes, his body relaxed, eyes on mine, he takes a sip of his drink, a gentle curve to his thick lips.

People would just say *good* or *fine* or possibly something much more positive, even if it wasn't true, but this is Blaze and I think he actually wants to know. The *truth*. Ugly or otherwise, I think he'd rather have it.

"Not great," I admit, vulnerable, but honest.

"What, that big fancy mansion of yours not all it's cracked up to be?" he half laughs, it sounds forced, maybe my answer made him feel awkward.

Warmth hits my cheeks again and I'm starting to wonder if I'm having body temperature control issues or if I'm genuinely this much of an embarrassing mess.

"Um, no, I, well it's fine," I stutter, frowning down at my hands, never knowing how to explain this part. Not even really to myself, "It's fine."

"Okay," he chuckles, a slightly bitter sound that makes me wince.

I look up at him then, a frown on his face as he studies his drink, tipping the cup this way and that, the liquid dancing with flames in the reflection.

"It's lonely."

The words are whispered, raw and pathetic, but true. So true that it hurts my chest to admit it. It's lonely because I couldn't make friends, kids teased me and picked on me, bullied me until I didn't want to go to school anymore, wouldn't go. I got home schooled, in isolation, no one but me and a tutor for eight hours a day, five days a week, four years of my life. I can play flute and piano and hold an okay tune, I know how to knit, crochet and cross stitch. I can speak three different languages fluently and I can run the London Marathon in under three hours.

But I don't know how to communicate without my palms starting to sweat, my cheeks heating and my mouth going dry. I don't know how to say thank you when someone holds a door for me because I'm worried someone's going to pay me more attention than I want, so instead I just look rude and entitled. I'm not allowed out of my house after dark without security, I've never had a boyfriend or a girlfriend, I've never had anyone except for myself, and I might be highly educated but it all means nothing to me in the grand scheme of things.

When you can't even hold a simple conversation without blacking out or having a panic attack, what are you really achieving in life?

Blaze's eyes lift, I can feel them on me, my own watery, I don't look. No one's ever sat down with me like this, just to talk, ask me how I am. I just follow orders and go through the motions.

"Rich ain't all its advertised as then, huh?"

I shake my head, still not looking at him, my insides cooling, everything in me starting to feel uncomfortable now.

I'm just a sad girl that torments herself.

"How about you?" I ask quietly, my head bowed, eyes flicking to his.

He's staring at his drink again, bringing the cup to his lips, he swallows, his throat working as he arches his neck, tipping the cup all the way up, emptying it, discarding the plastic to the thin carpet at our feet. I look down at my own drink, knowing I absolutely should not be thinking about taking even a sip of whatever it is. But I wonder if it might help my nerves, make me relax just a tiny fraction, enough to not be boring, be the sad, weird girl, that flinches with touch.

I take a tentative sip, screwing my face up at the bitterness, I swallow it down, barely enough to properly taste, but I'm grateful when Blaze reaches out, his hand covering the top of the cup, fingers curling over its edges. He takes it from me, placing it down on the floor too, out of my reach, and I'm silently thankful he does so.

I'm not supposed to drink.

He twists in place, his knee brushing the outside of my thigh, his stare boring holes into the side of my face.

"You don't want to ask about me," he rasps in response, the darkness that usually unsettles me making me feel a little less exposed under his scrutinising stare.

I glance up, a question in my eyes that he gives a single shake of his head to.

"Did you…"

I trail off, not really wanting to ask the question, not wanting to know, but he knows what it is I'm asking.

Our secret in the past.

"No."

I nod slowly at the confirmation, swallowing hard, a trickle of cold rolling down my spine.

"Why did you want to know?"

I look up then, his dark eyes on me, soft. The space we're in, quiet, flickering orange glowing across the wall, flames from outside the window reflecting.

"I didn't want you to get in trouble," I whisper the confession, everything inside this quiet room sounds too loud, too much, like I'll ruin whatever's happening here if I speak too loudly.

"No one will ever know what happened, pretty girl."

His thumb sweeps across the scar beneath my eye again, my eyes fluttering closed, like settling butterflies atop my cheeks.

"No one touches you."

It's him whispering this time. The fragile atmosphere we find ourselves in, something, it seems, could be easily broken. Currently, neither one of us wants to break it. The tips of his fingers slide gently into my hair, thumb resting over my scar. A shiver wracks through me, touch feeling like fire razing across my skin. Goosebumps smatter, raising and running down my throat, my arms, across my chest. My bottom lip trembles as he slides his fingers into my hair, the palm of his large hand smothering the side of my face, over my ear, warmth and smoke.

"I don't want anyone to," I profess almost silently.

"What about me, Ember?" he asks the question so softly, like he's that eighteen year old boy again, tall and gangly, with holes in his t-shirts.

I think about his question, feel his heat on my face, his rough but almost delicate hold on my cheek. In this moment, can I give him a little of my trust? He had it once upon a time. It's been ten years since I saw him last, since he would knock on my front door and walk me to school. Like a big brother would, well, one that wasn't like mine anyway, Danny didn't ever walk me to school, it's why Blaze did it.

Decision made, I settle into the hold, my instincts telling me to run and relax all at the same time. I force it all down, think of the boy that protected me, and feel myself lean in deeper. The pads of his fingers gently massage my scalp, his entire hand hidden beneath my thick curls. He turns me to face him, my eyes still closed, I feel him lean closer, his breath on my other cheek. The lengths of his hair tickling against my skin. I tremble, his other hand going to one of mine. His fingers slotting between my parted ones, his palm over the back of my hand, he squeezes my hand gently, forcing me to release the death grip I have on my knee.

He pulls our hands away slightly, turning my palm up in his, his fingers closing between mine. He flexes his grip, my hand feeling tiny inside his, my skin prickles, but I sort of like it. His warm breath on the side of my throat, he presses his cheek to my own, rough stubble sharp. A slow measured movement, created not to spook, not to make me uncomfortable. I feel safe, warm, calm.

"You don't like to be touched." A statement, one I shake my head to, just a singular movement of agreement. "What happened, Emmy?" his soft lips brush over my cheek, my breath rushing out of me, the genuine concern in his question makes my heart thump. "I won't hurt you."

It's those words…

Those words feel like a lie.

My eyes snap open. He draws his face away from the side of mine, a teasing curve to his lips, bringing himself face to face with me, so close I almost go cross-eyed looking at him. Our noses brush, my breath stills in my lungs.

"Not in a way you won't like," he rasps, dark and heavy, thick with something that makes my stomach muscles tight.

Breath rushes out of me, I lick my lips, swallow the lump in my throat. My free hand slides from my thigh, coming up between us, splaying over his chest, the pad of my middle finger resting in the hollow of his throat. His heart hammers beneath my palm, solid, strong, *real*. I bite my lip, nibbling on the inside of it, my eyes flicking between his, so dark, and wide, locked on me like he wants to devour me, and I don't think I hate the idea. His high cheekbones shadowing his cheeks, carving them deeper into his wide square jaw. He pulls his lip ring into his mouth, his teeth clicking against the metal as he chews.

My finger traces the tiny piece of bare skin it rests upon, smoothing over the base of his throat. Our eyes never wavering from one another. I wonder what we're doing, what we're waiting for, why I'm allowing anyone to touch me at all, why *I* am voluntarily touching someone. It all just strangely feels like it should be this way.

"I'm not a gentle man," he whispers, lips caressing mine with his words, his minty breath, tinged with the alcohol he drank. "But I could try," a pause, drawn out, my breath held tight in my chest, I wait for him to finish, "for you." I shiver, my eyes desperately wanting to close but not wanting to look away. "I think there's a reason you're here tonight."

I blink then, breaking the hold he somehow tangled me in, I pull back, my gaze dropping between us, seeing our hands entangled together. His darker skin to my pale, I look pasty in comparison, unhealthy, deprived of the sun. Which would be accurate, I never really leave my room, let alone my house. I get driven to work in the back of a blacked out vehicle, escorted to and from the door at drop off and pick up. It was my request to start with, after what happened to me, when I was taken. It's why I don't like the dark, after being locked up in the boot of a car, a hood over my head, everything that happened after.

The things I remember.

The things I don't.

"Hey," Blaze's hand on my face shifts, finger and thumb smoothing their way to my chin, lifting my gaze back to his. "What just happened?"

I lick my lips, mouth dry, skin hot, "sorry."

"I didn't ask for an apology, pretty girl. I asked you what happened, where'd you go, what were you thinking about? Is it me?" his questions are unhurried, asked slowly, to give me time to think about them, answer.

A crease forms between my brows, unsure how to articulate real words in the moment when all I can feel is how his rough skin feels against mine. His heat, more and also less than the temperature of the room, the fire outside, flames in the cold night's air. I feel hot and cold, dizzy and insane and I think I just want to stop thinking about it all. The only way I know how to get even just a moment's reprieve is to cut and cut and cut. My breath holds in my lungs, a cool sweat prickling the nape of my neck beneath my thick length of blonde curls.

"It's not you," I say as breath rushes out of me.

"It's not me," an echoing statement, something like self-reassurance.

A sinister tilt hits his devilish lips and then they're on mine.

He presses his mouth to mine, the cool metal of his lip ring shocking against my hot skin. His tongue instantly licking over the seam of my lips, I'm frozen, in surprise, his mouth moving over mine and I'm just motionless for a second. He pulls back, his fingers laced through mine squeezing tightly, his dark eyes flickering between my own.

"You don't want to kiss me."

I blush, taking in a shuddery breath, panic sparking in my chest.

"It's not that," I say quietly, everything in me so, so hot, I'm surely smouldering.

"Okay…" he shakes his head, like he's clearing his thoughts, a cloud that's settled there, and then his gaze is snapping back to mine. "*Oh,* oh."

Heat flushes in my cheeks, his very correct assumption, realisation, my shame. A blush scorches my skin, racing up my throat, across my chest, skin surely a bright, blood red beneath my white shirt.

"Ember."

I squeeze my eyes shut, tears burning the back of them, I absolutely should not have come here.

"Was that…" Blaze clears his throat, his words cautious, like he's afraid speaking my own truth back to me will hurt me. "Is this your first kiss?" a delicately spoken question, one that twists and grinds my insides violently.

This shouldn't be a thing. Like, I'm twenty-two, but I'm not normal. At all. I could say yes, which may or may not be a lie. I could say no, which is also possibly one or the other. The sad truth of it is is I don't know.

"I don't know," the words escape me a little too quickly, but slowly, opening my eyes, I drag my gaze back up to his.

His brow furrowed, lips pursed, his nostrils flare,

his grip on my hand, the hold on my face, all of it tightening to the point of pain.

"What does that mean?"

Licking my lips, I whisper, "I got taken." It feels like a pressure inside my skull starts to release. "And I was drugged, and I don't know what happened to me."

I wince, his finger and thumb squeezing my chin too, too hard, before he's letting go completely. Dropping my hand with a thud to my thigh, his hand on my face tearing away, I almost fall forward with the surprising loss of contact. I didn't realise just how much I was leaning into his hold. For someone who can't usually stand to be touched, I suddenly feel like a block of ice without it.

Blaze throws himself up off of the bed, fast pacing across the carpet, back and forth before the window, muttering under his breath. His dark silhouette shadowing the wall, the flames from outside lighting one half of him, making him look like some sort of fire born hell demon. He tugs on his hair, breathes hard through his nose.

I don't move, don't speak, unsure what it is that's actually happening here. He stops dead centre of the dark room, head dropping back, he pinches the bridge of his nose, face angled towards the ceiling, he sighs heavily. And then he's striding towards the wall, his fist colliding with it over and over, his back heaving with his heavy breaths. He roars as he pummels it, making me shrink back, but I watch enraptured, ears numb to the sounds as I see something dark smear across the light coloured wall.

My feet move of their own accord, unconsciously, because I'm suddenly standing right behind him and I don't know how I got here. One of my hands goes to the centre of his shoulder blades. My palm splaying over the top of his spine, he stills at the contact, I'm still a foot away when his head drops forward, both forearms braced on the wall by the sides of his head, fingers curled into fists. I step into him, put a little more weight into my touch, make sure he really feels me.

It's like an electric current whips through me, the shudder at touch, I'm not sure I don't like it as much as it just feels foreign. His heat scorching through his hoodie, my palm feeling slick at the contact. I can feel his heart thudding against my hand, beating erratically, his lungs working overtime as his breathing continues to heave.

"Blaze."

He spins around, hands going to my waist, he turns us both, thrusting me against the wall so hard, my head thuds against the brickwork, my eyes rattling in their sockets. He blocks me in, hips pinning me to the wall, his head dipped, eyes closed, I don't know what he's thinking, I squirm in his hold. Not liking to be blocked in, cornered, unable to escape. I glance to my right, eyeing the door that feels too far away. What would I do if I were free, would I even leave?

No.

Blaze breathes down the side of my throat, his dark brown curls falling forward, silken soft against my temple. His rough stubble grazing my jaw, tip of his nose against the lobe of my ear. His breathing starts to slow when I stop struggling, still tense, but not actively trying to escape any more. Somehow starting to like the feeling of being held by him, even as the skin beneath my clothes itches and burns.

"I don't like the thought of someone touching you," it feels like something raw and true, an unavoidable confession between us, somewhat vulnerable, and I don't think a man like Blaze McCoy is ever seen to be vulnerable.

"No one is touching me," I whisper, his head still dipped, hands on my waist so tight my ribs bow, he pushes a knee between my thighs. "Only you," it feels dangerous, like the words could catch fire and burn us both.

He growls, low and deep, primal, something monstrous, animalistic, raw. I feel like I'm burning, blistering, smouldering, an inferno ripping through me as he says, "only me. Say it again."

"Only you," I breathe immediately without hesitation, my breath ruffling the dark curls on the side of his head.

He draws back, eyes darting between mine, I swallow and then his lips come crashing down on mine. I don't know what I'm doing, what I should do, what's even happening in this moment. But he's rough, forceful, his tongue lashes over my closed lips, prodding at my teeth for entrance. I part my lips and his tongue comes licking into my mouth, long, rapid licks of his tongue over mine. And then I find myself kissing him back, my lips move gently, tenderly, an eagerness equal to his but less practised.

He groans, the sound vibrating through my mouth, over my teeth, down my throat. I moan, breathing him in, one of his hands going to my lower spine. He pulls my pelvis flush against his, my back arching away from the wall. His lips caress mine, it's hard and powerful, rough and demanding, hot, so hot, I feel as if I'm going to combust. We're panting hard, breaths mingling, his taste on my tongue, smoky and spicy sweet, making me shiver. His hands grope over my skin where he holds me tight, and my body rejects and invites it all at the same time. Blaze tears his lips from mine, my breathing hard in the small space between us.

"Fuck," he murmurs, a small tilt to his lips. He eyes me quietly, pecking at my lips once more, his nose brushing over mine like a feathered caress, "that was your first kiss," he murmurs, informing me, puffy lips stroking my swollen ones with each word.

I nod, his hand sliding up my spine, crook of his elbow beneath my arm, hand sliding into the back of my hair, fingers roughly kneading the back of my head. I let my eyes fall shut, my body loosen against every instinct I have that screams not to. His other arm sliding around me until I'm wrapped up in his arms, flush against his body, no way to escape, my limbs entangled with his. His knee between my thighs, arms tight, my own moving and sliding to fit to him, one between us, resting against his broad chest, the other, my fingers latching over his strong forearm. To push him away, to pull him in closer, I can't decide, my brain flitting between scenarios, outcomes.

"I want to fuck you," it's a harsh whisper, a bite to the words. "I can be gentle, I'll *try* to be gentle, but, Ember…"

I look up, his face so, so close, my tongue could lick across his thick lips without any effort at all, to taste, to breathe in, consume, devour. I don't understand what's happening to me when I realise I'm waiting for him to continue because I just want to say *yes*.

"Don't make me," it's a plea, dark, it ignites the most vulnerable part of my soul.

I don't speak, there are no words to seal my fate, instead there's just a kiss.

His big hands are tugging at my shirt, our lips only severing their connection for him to tear it over my head. My fingers pull on his hoodie, drawing it up and over his head along with his black t-shirt beneath. His skin is scorching, scalding to the point of blistering as I trace my hands up and over his flesh. I'm nervous, cautious, unsure what I should be doing when he groans against my mouth, his lip ring mashing against my bottom teeth as he bites and sucks on my lips.

His fingers find my jeans, expertly releasing the button and zipper, his mouth breaking free of mine, fingers curling around my hips.

"Take me out, hold me in your tiny fucking hand and squeeze hard, pretty girl."

I exhale hard, trembling even harder, his teeth find my jaw, biting and nipping his way down, his lips sucking at the sting, one hand curling over his shoulder, the other between us, the heat of him scalding as my fingers curl over the waistband of his joggers and boxers, the tops of my fingers igniting as they move beneath the fabric.

Blaze grabs my face suddenly in both hands, fingers smoothing over my head, down the length of my hair, before coming back to my cheeks. He holds my face delicately, like I'm something fragile he doesn't want to be heavy handed with. But his sinful mouth is quite the opposite.

His tongue delves in my mouth the same time I move my hand beneath his clothes. I don't know what to do, but I follow his earlier instructions. He's huge, in comparison to my small hand, I can hardly wrap my fingers around him but I do. One of his hands falls from my face, moving to his joggers, he shoves the material down, freeing his hard cock, my hand wrapped around it. I squeeze tightly, his flesh, hot and hard, leaking at the tip, a hiss spearing between his teeth, he nips my lower lip, panting into my mouth.

His big body crushing me to the wall, hips thrusting into my hand. I squeeze tightly, releasing him, my grip still firm, I run my hand down his length, feel a vein in the underside of his dick throbbing against my hand, I trace it with the tip of my finger, fumbling my movements, but he doesn't seem to mind.

Blaze takes my lips in a scorching kiss, devouring me, my insides alight with want. I find myself exploring him, his cock growing impossibly harder in my grip. He groans, moaning heavily between pants as I flex my hold on him. His cock weeps, wetting my thumb and fingers, I pull it down his length, his fingers biting into my skin harder, bruising. He thrusts into my hand harder, my fingers slipping and sliding up and down his shaft now, his hot breath desperate against the side of my throat. He grips my waist, squeezing my bones, he flips us so his back's to the wall instead, and then he's walking me backwards, our teeth and lips never severing.

The back of my thighs hit the small mattress, my bum dropping to the pale sheets it's dressed with, my hand falling away from his pulsing length. Our lips break apart too, but then he's crawling over the top of me, his mouth reconnecting with mine, hunger and desperation thick in the air between us. My hands walking me backwards until the back of my skull is colliding with the wooden headboard and Blaze is dragging me down the bed under him. He smothers me with his body, and I find my skin starting to crawl until his weight drops onto me, and although he's heavy and solid, and his muscles dig into my bones, I find I like it better.

"I'm going to be so good to you, pretty girl," he says over my mouth, my own swallowing his words without processing them.

He grabs my hand, yanks it between us, guides me back into locking my fingers back around him. He squeezes his hand over mine, working himself using me, guiding me to how he likes it without spoken words, his other hand tangled in my hair.

When I'm doing everything exactly as he wants, squeezing so tight, I would think it's got to hurt, rolling my thumb around his crown, dragging precum down his length. He rears up onto his knees, between my spread thighs, my body moving up with him so I can keep my fist on his cock. Not daring to let go, do anything without his instruction, permission. I also don't want to give myself time to think about what it is I'm doing, no wanting to change my mind, use rational thought and logic to stop me from what is inevitably a mistake.

His hands go to my jeans, shoving them down, pulling at the fabric so hard they crack under his grip, he shoves me to the bed, fighting with the stiff denim, throwing them to the floor as he tears them down my legs, removing them along with my boots, leaving me in just my underwear. He drops forward again, his bare chest decorated in tattoo designs I can't see, pressing against mine. His fingers delve into the cups of my bra, twisting and plucking my rock hard nipples. His mouth sucks down my throat and I know he's leaving his mark on me but I can't find it in myself to care.

And if I wake up in the morning, back in my bed, bruise free, then I'll know I'm just as fucked up as everyone says I am.

My free hand finds his head, fingers twisting in his loose, dark curls, applying pressure to the back of his head, keeping him clutched to my chest as he runs his tongue across my skin. Goosebumps erupting over my flesh, the heat of his breath blowing over the trail his tongue leaves. He works his way down my body, my arm stretching as far as it can to remain locked on his cock. He pushes me off, diving down between my legs, he mouths at my pussy and I arch up off the bed, hips involuntarily bucking against his face.

"You smell so fucking good," he growls, the sound rattling up his chest, I don't have time to process anything as he tears my knickers free.

The cotton carves painfully into my skin before it rips free, the seams cracking and ripping, and then his mouth is over me. His tongue fucking into my cunt, lips massaging my hot flesh, he drags his tongue up the length of me, sucking on my clit, the metal of his lip ring making me tremble as it snags over my swollen clit.

I pant, my grip in his hair tightening, my other hand joining, twisting in his thick strands. His stubble grazes over the inside of my thighs, rubbing my skin raw as he buries his face in my cunt. He grips my thighs in a punishing hold, fingertips gouging at my skin, bruising, biting, attacking. He traces his fingers over the scars there, deep, jagged, fresh and old, but he doesn't stop, doesn't ask, but I know he feels them because he touches them with something that feels like reverence.

Every part of him overwhelms me and I succumb to the pleasure as he closes his mouth over me, his teeth biting down on my clit. I howl out my release, my legs vibrating in his hold, joints turning to jelly, and then he flips us.

My head spinning, legs straddling his thighs, I peer down at him, my bra askew, breasts spilling out of the cups, a strap hanging down one arm. Blaze looks up at me with a feral kind of hunger. Something almost horrifying about it as the reflection of the bonfire flames light up one half of his face. His bare cock is thick and long between us, veins protruding along it as it jumps in place, precum from the tip smearing over his lower abs. Glistening in the flickering light, my eyes locking in on it as it bobs against his belly.

"You can be in control, pretty girl," he rasps the lie, my stomach twisting as I peer down into his dark eyes, black as the night's sky, endless depths of ebony. "I'll guide you," it's breathy and rife with need, lighting my insides up.

His hand covers one of mine, shaky in his grasp, he watches me, our eyes on each other's as he guides me back to his cock. The silken skin pulled tight around his swollen length, my fingers curling around his base, his other hand harsh on my hip, gesturing me up onto my knees. I move as he does, his strong hold on my hip helping lift me so I'm hovering above him. I lick my lips, his other hand, the one over mine, moves us together until the swollen head of his cock is nestled at my entrance. I heave in breath after breath, my eyes never leaving his, his fingertips biting into my hip, he starts to force me down.

My knees lock, his cock just breaching my entrance, the slick head of him just inside of me, my walls involuntarily clamp down, around nothing but an expectation, when I realise what the problem is.

"I don't…" I pause, my chest heaving. "I want to be on the bottom," the words rush out of me, nerves racing through my bones.

Blaze shakes his head, sitting up, clutching me to him, my hand still squeezing his cock between us, he takes my face in his hands, my entire body flush to his, my hand trapped between us.

"If you're on top, you're in control," he whispers the words, but I'm not sure he means to.

Raising my eyes to his, I chew on my lip, grip on his cock making him groan as I roll my thumb over his tip.

"I want to be on the bottom," I breathe the words that seal my fate.

Blaze flips us, my back hitting the mattress, his body smothering me. His teeth latch onto my bottom lip, hands all over my body, he gives me no time to second guess anything because his cock is inside of me in one brutal thrust. He hits the tip of his dick into the entrance of my cervix like a battering ram that's on fire. I curl up beneath him, my body writhing and arching, pain ripping through my spinal cord.

A rush of heat tears through me, my cunt clenching around him, desperately trying to stretch to him, mould to his thickness, his length, as he holds still inside me. I burn and smoulder, dense ash falling down around us, keeping us inside a fragile moment of fire. A glass bauble of lust, passion, need and want, shaken up like a sinister snow globe, but filled with smoke and flames.

Blaze licks up the front of my throat, nipping along my collarbone, down my chest, my thighs burn, my chest heaving. My heart swells then implodes as his lips find their way back to mine.

"I want you to fucking bow beneath me, pretty girl, fucking scream for me."

An order I don't need to try to follow, one that unwillingly is pulled from me, his hands splay either side of my head, his bare chest glistening in the flickering light, slick with sweat. He grunts and groans as I claw at his back, a scream tearing through my teeth. Wanting to peel away his skin and flesh in the same way I want to remove my own. But I can't decide if it's because I want us to be nearer, closer, wrapped together as one or if it's because I hate to be touched, but I can't decide because the hellfire lashing through me feels like blissful brutal rapture.

"Say my name," he chants the demand over and over in my ear, his cock slamming in and out of me like a punishment.

My echo back something similar, "*Blaze, Blaze, Blaze.*"

Teeth pull at my lobe, his mouth nibbling and sucking down my throat, along my jaw, he pulls my hair, tongue lashing over my skin. I'm so covered in him, I don't know where he stops and I begin. I want to crawl my way inside of him, claw him close, carve my way inside his chest, bury my pain in him. Let him devour and destroy me.

Cock thrusting into me, harsh and ruthless, his hips smack into mine and it almost feels cruel until heat rushes up my spine, my legs squeezing around him, and I come. His cock buried deep inside of me, I strangle his dick, my muscles and walls clamping and closing in around him. He groans, a sound falling free from his throat, reminiscent of a wounded animal, primal and rough.

He drops his forehead to mine, slowing his pace, dragging his throbbing cock almost lazily in and out of me. He stares down into my eyes, big and wide and dark, if I look into them long enough I'm pretty sure they could swallow me whole.

"I never expected this," he says against my lips, peppering featherlight kisses over my swollen mouth, the tip of my nose. "I can't believe it," he laughs softly, disbelief, something like awe, making my cheeks flush hotter.

One of his splayed palms still supporting him, the other lifting to my face, cupping my cheek, thumb smoothing over the apple of my cheekbone. His cock moves inside of me, our bodies connected, my chest heaving, his slowing, more controlled. It makes me panic, but then he's pushing in so deep, his hand leaving my face, gripping behind my knee, twisting my leg up to wrap around his lower spine. He dips back down, his breath mingling with mine.

Licking his lips, he says, "I'm taking it slow now, you gunna let me enjoy you, pretty girl?"

I'm nodding before he finishes his question, his body rocking against mine, slow, but hard snaps of his hips. His mouth makes love to me, his tongue and his cock no longer fucking into me, but gliding, slippery and wet, a blazing inferno of heat searing between us. I feel such a connection to him, he's saying so much without using any words at all. He kisses me and I kiss him back, and then he's clinging onto me, his arms wrapping behind my back as I come again. This time it's not a carnal explosion, it's slow, warming carefully, a steady sizzling between us, a gentle wave lapping over me instead of a tidal wave.

He thrusts into me one final brutal time, a suppressed roaring through his clenched teeth, he fills me with his cum. I feel him fill me, his cock pulsing and swelling inside of me, my walls clamping down around him, he paints my insides with him. Then he's pulling me closer, my face burying inside his chest, his cock still twitching inside of me. His hand strokes down my thigh, pulled over his hip, he kisses my head, pushes my curls back from my face, sweat slick on my neck. He runs his tongue up my throat, suckling on my jaw.

"Stay with me," he murmurs against my cheek, kissing me over and over.

Blaze's hand is smoothing over the crown of my head as I nod my agreement. Holding me so tight I can hardly breathe, my skin is on fire, flames trying to flay it free from my bones, but I like it. It feels good, and strange and like I never want it to end.

But even I know that all good things must come to an end.

And sometimes a lot sooner than you think.

CHAPTER 7
FLINT

The darkness feels like home, wrapping me up in its shadows. My blood boils beneath skin that smells like fire. Hot, charring, familiar. I stalk through the tall crops, swaying and swishing roughly in the harsh November wind. I know where I'll find my Phoenix, playing away with his dolls in the darkness. I walk through the field blind. Nothing but the occasional burst of moonlight lighting my path, there's a buzzing in my ears, adrenaline, a fight broiling in the centre of my chest.

A need to take that woman away from my older brother. A need to make her know she was never safe, no matter how he pretends to charm her, lure her, break her. We were built for ruin, not fairytales.

I have an itch, a need to show Phoenix that I own him tonight, and no matter how many people he makes smile, *hers* will be the only one I'll count.

I wonder how long it will take for Blaze to let us have her.

I'll make her cry, Nix will make her smile.

It'll all be over too soon.

I still my bootsteps, head tilting to one side, a quiet cry carrying on the breeze. I switch direction. Carving a quick right, back towards the abandoned Halloween maze, I feel my pace pick up, the swishing and swooshing of the tall crops and their leaves rushes around me like a breaking wave.

Approaching the edge at the back of the carved out maze, I hear a whimper, a huff, a small grunt, a thump. A smile flashes over my lips, mouth pulling up at the corners, knowing exactly what I'll find. Watching between the thick plants, Phoenix dips low, grabbing an ankle and arranging the body upon a pyre, darkness is already covering their front, even in the little light from the moon I can see he's almost done.

Enthralled, I watch him work, I don't doubt he can sense me nearby, but I don't disturb him. Watching his shirtless torso bend and flex, muscles tight and drawn beneath his golden, suntanned skin. His blonde hair like a halo atop his head, the cold wind tousling its length across his face, he pushes it back, wiping a forearm over his forehead, back of his hand over his chin. Dark eyes glance up, to the dark night's sky above, his chest heaving but his breaths deep and even, he cracks his neck, left to right. Resuming shifting the other bodies at his feet.

He places them one by one, upon the wood stacks, a dug out trench around its base, a true professional when it comes to controlling fire. I would not have been so careful, it's why I'm not allowed to play with flames unattended anymore. Pyromania is a mental illness, dangerous in its entirety, but one I never want cured.

Phoenix scuffs his boot across the dewy ground, the crops cleared for the maze. A slow fog drifts around his ankles, his hot breath fogging before his face. Nix continues arranging his dolls, settling each one of them perfectly, in the exact position he likes, arranging. I watch him work with careful hands, his fingers gentle, manoeuvring feet and hands, arms and legs, all with a delicate grace.

I'm patient, I want his attention, if I distract him before he's done, I won't get it fully. There are ways he has to do things, perform, position, every-thing needing to be crafted *just* right.

I step through the tall harvest, a little cough, throat clearing, to announce my official arrival. Phoenix turns slowly, his sculpted chest glistening like the galaxies twinkling above us, hidden beneath torrents of dense cloud, the moonlight licking over his skin, gifting him an angelic glow. His dark eyes rove up onto my ice blues, too great a distance between us, I want to close it, rush forward, bend him over, make him moan and bow beneath me, but I don't. Instead, I step forward cautiously, surveying the area around me, thick trails of blood, bodies dragged through puddles of crimson, sweeping their way to their final resting place.

Phoenix isn't picky with his dolls, as long as he can make them smile, he'll have anyone. There's no right or wrong in his eyes, only sadness that he feels an incessant need to cure.

Sadness is the world's greatest sickness.

Phoenix only wants to correct that.

My approach is slow, feet not bothering to avoid the mess, I step right up into him, pressing my chest to his. My hand cradles the back of his skull, only an inch separating us in height, my six-five to his six-four, I dip my head, lips brushing up the side of his blood speckled neck, tasting salt and copper. Other hand cupping the side of his throat, his cool skin slick with a fine layer of sweat, I breathe him in, a sharp iron tingeing his crisp apple and smoked birch scent.

"Would you like help?" I breathe into his ear, teeth grazing the shell.

Slowly, one of his large hands comes up in the small space between us, silence all around, my heart rate settles as his palm slides over it, cool skin, painted red, rests over the top of my t-shirt. My arms prick with goosebumps, cold air whipping around us, reminding us we're outside, in the elements, not locked inside an invisible bubble created just for us.

Slowly, he shakes his head against me, one singular movement. His other hand comes up, fisting in my cotton t-shirt, tugging me closer, our bodies touching everywhere. Our hips aligned, his cock thickening beneath his tight jeans, pressing against my own. He breathes me in, slow and deep, my scent calming and familiar, helping bring him back down from his high.

I ground him in the same way he grounds me.

"Blaze has a girl," I breathe the information into his ear, tongue lapping over his lobe. "I think we should take her," I breathe softly, the words a golden thread, something he can latch onto. "She looks sad," I confess, it makes me frown just a little, her big blue eyes were too glassy for happiness. "We could play with her together."

"When Blaze is done," he whispers, his answer methodical, voice a soft, ghostlike caress against the cool skin of my neck.

Silently, I nod, latching my lips over his pulse, sucking lightly, he arches into me. Grip tightening in my shirt, his palm still pressed to my chest, his fingers flex, their tips digging in. A flare of heat thrashes through me when he shifts his hips, my knee pushing between his thighs.

Pulse in his throat hammering erratically against my palm, my thumb stroking down the front of his neck, over his Adam's apple, stopping in the hollow of his throat. I kiss his cheekbone, over his closed eyelids, down his nose, my lips finding his, he kisses me back, our tongues tangling lazily, like we have all the time in the world. We do, because if anyone were to disturb this, our moment, what we do together in the safety of shadows, I would slaughter them and then fuck Nix in their blood.

Phoenix's sticky palm slides up my chest, gripping my throat. Fingers flexing over my pulse, his head drops back, a delicate smile on his pink lips, cupid's bow carved deep, he looks like a fucking cherub.

Gripping his throat, him gripping mine, we pull on each other at the same time. Our lips colliding, teeth crashing, tongues licking into mouths. Mine sliding over his, grip on his throat angling him, I bite into his lower lip, tongue bar clacking over his teeth as I do.

We're manic, tearing at each other's clothes, clawing skin, biting lips, pulling hair. I wrench his head back as his hands find the waistband of my jeans. His bloodied fingers slipping inside, wrapping around my cock like firm silk, I pant against his temple, my head dipped, neck curled into him. He runs his hand up my length, my abs tightening with heat, an inferno blazing to life in my lower belly, lighting a fire inside my chest. My heart thrashes like it's on fire, desperate to break free of its boned prison, ribs curling in, puncturing their way into my dark soul.

Phoenix squeezes me in his hand, my cock pulsing, he flicks his thumb over the piercing in my tip, making me groan. Head dropping back, he expertly smears precum down my shaft, the tips of his fingers grazing over my balls, they draw up, tingles racing across the bottom of my spine. I grip his waist, spinning him around, his hand leaving me. My teeth delving into the nape of his neck, I bite down until I draw blood to the surface, sucking his flesh, but not breaking skin.

His breaths panting, my arm tight around his waist, I tug him sharply into me, my jeans open, cock begging to sink into him, I trace my free hand down the front of his chest, his jeans hanging open, half sliding down his hips. I glide the heel of my hand down his abs, the tight muscles jumping against my touch. Fingers dip into his loose boxers, his huge cock, thick and weeping, twitches beneath the calloused skin of my long fingers. I grip him tight, strangling him in my hold, easing down his foreskin, middle finger tracing the thick vein thrumming in the underside of his length.

"Set them on fire, Flint," he hushes out, his voice so fucking delicate it makes my balls ache.

"You're such a good boy," I rasp against his throat, the moan slipping through his teeth almost a whimper.

I let him go, spin to face the pyre, my eyes adjusting to the darkness, I see three bodies stacked upon it, laid out like they're sleeping, smiles carved into each of their faces. A bludgeoning to the first one's head, a stab wound to the chest of the other and a second smile sliced across a third one's throat.

I cock my head at that one, Nix gliding up beside me, he too, tilts his head, admiring the view. His eyes home in on the third man, my gaze on his reaction out the corner of my eye, his plush lips pull up on one side.

"That one was extra sad," he informs me, almost silently.

I nod, step forward, free an engraved lighter from my pocket, flames etched into the sleek black metal, reds and oranges I can't see in the dark, but know they're there. I flick the top, flame dancing in the breeze, Nix tossing me a short piece of old fence, I light it up. A blaze scorching it instantly, lighter fluid already on one end, I toss it onto the pyre and watch as it erupts into flames. The excitement that pulses through me, at starting a fire, is unexplainable, but I feel it soothe me just a fraction as the red flames lick up towards the dark sky.

Phoenix tears me back, my feet scrabbling beneath me, and then his tongue is in my mouth, hands all over my body, he shoves my jeans and boxers down, my raging hard cock bobbing free. He drops to his knees, his hot mouth closing around my tip, tongue running up my length. He fists my balls, squeezing and massaging as he swallows me whole. His dark eyes locked on mine, pretty pink mouth stretched around my length, one of my hands in his hair, the other finding his throat, he sucks and slurps.

Spit running down his chin, my cock pulsing against his tongue, pierced tip hitting the back of his throat. He sucks me in, hollowed cheeks and lashing tongue. He keeps his eyes on mine the entire time and just when I can feel myself about to come, I pull out of his mouth. Tear him up to his feet by my hold on his throat, kissing him so hard I taste blood on my tongue. I spin him in my hold, shoving down his jeans, boxers dropping with them.

The heat from the fire, the smell of burning flesh rife in the air, I push between his shoulder blades, fingers curling over his shoulder, he bends forward, hands splayed on his knees. My other hand grabs one of his firm cheeks, pulling his flesh harshly to one side, I spit on his tight hole. One of his hands leaves his knee, moving up behind him, coming between us. Fisting my dick, he tugs it closer. Releasing his shoulder, I shuffle forward at his silent instruction, palm his other cheek, massaging his flesh. I spit again, his hand leaving me, quickly replaced with my own, I run my fingers down my shaft, pump myself, spit on my cock.

Everything inside of me screaming to take, take, take.

And then I'm lining myself up with his entrance, my swollen tip pushing past his tight ring of muscle. My fingers curl around his hips, heels of my hands and thumbs still separating his cheeks, easing myself inside of him. Bottoming out, I pull him up to stand, back flush with my chest, my head going over his shoulder. A hand splaying over his lower abs, one curling around his throat, my grip flexing, I bite the side of his neck. His muscles squeeze tight around me, my breath stuttering through my teeth, I tentatively draw out, thrust back in, slowly picking up speed until I'm fucking him at a brutal pace.

Sliding my hand lower down his belly, fingers finding his cock, I curl around his hot shaft, pumping him with long, firm strokes. He grunts, turning his chin up towards me, teeth catching the underside of my jaw, he suckles along the bone as I thrust inside of him. I fuck into him so hard it makes my teeth rattle inside my skull, my hand working in a tight corkscrew around him. Flames from our fire spitting and hissing, his wide, dark eyes looking up into mine. I kiss him hard, nothing soft or gentle as my teeth attack his tongue, sucking it into my mouth.

I squeeze his throat tight, cutting off his air, he stiffens beneath me, his hard, hot cock fucking into my hand with every smack of my hips forcing him forward, my dick punishing him from behind. Our teeth crash, his tongue fucking into my mouth, I groan as his hot cum splashes over my fist. Knuckles blanching white, I squeeze him hard, slowing my pace, his body tensing around me. One final thrust has me finishing inside of him, coating his insides with my release. Fingers dropping from his throat, splaying over his erratic heart, tight chest muscles heaving beneath my palm as he desperately sucks in air.

"I want to do that again," I tell him greedily, hunger in my words that are abruptly cut off.

"No, put your dicks away, we have shit to do. Both of you."

Top lip curling over my upper lip, a snarl rips free from my throat, I tear my softening cock out of Phoenix, shoving him behind me, animal instinct telling me to protect my mate. Blaze stands unde-terred at an opening in the maze, we're in a dead end corner so there's only the one way in. His hands are shoved in his pockets, reflection of our fire dancing across him, bathing him in orange light, his features morphing into the devil himself.

He stares at me with dark eyes, brows pinched tight, his gaze flicks over my shoulder, onto the fire, we can do whatever the fuck we want on Guy Fawkes and Blaze will clean it up. That's the deal. It's what we work so fucking hard for all year, a night to blow off steam. I get to burn shit, Nix gets to make sad dolls smile, Cole gets control. And Blaze, my older, adopted brother, well, he gets to *play*.

"We're going to play a game."

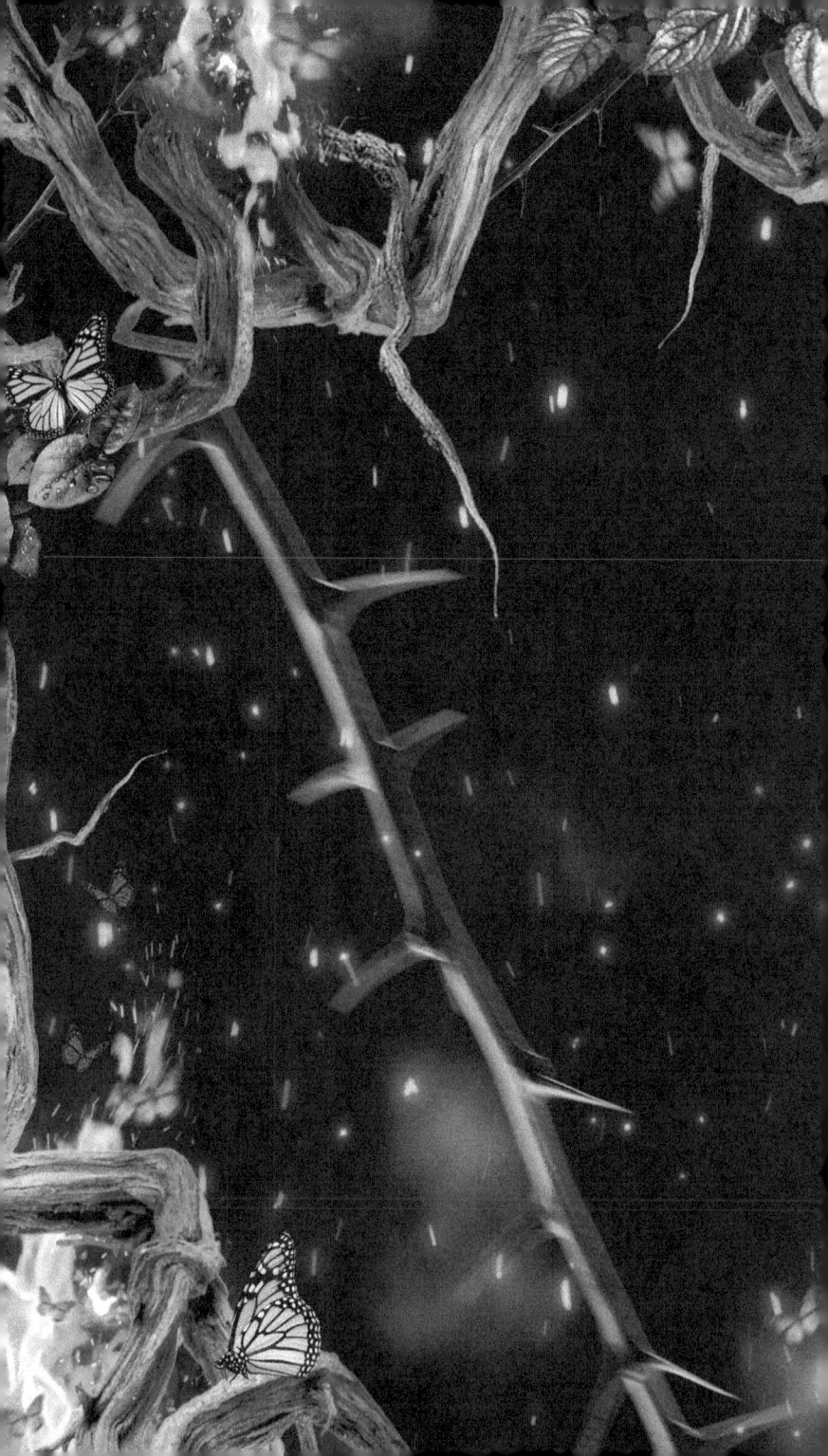

The first thing I realise is how cold I am. The second thing I realise is why. I don't have any clothes on. The third is that the bonfire is out, the room, despite the curtains being open, is dense darkness. And the final thing I realise, with pain in my chest and blood on my thighs, is I have been fucking ditched.

It shouldn't hurt.

It shouldn't mean anything.

It shouldn't make my eyes hot with unshed tears.

But it does all of those things anyway.

I practically crawl around on the floor, in the hunt for my clothes. My bra still skewed on my chest, I tuck my breasts inside the cups, right the straps, straighten the clip in the back. I find my jeans, boots more or less still tucked up inside of them, I pull it all on, tie my laces, tug them too tight but enjoy the pinch of pain in the tops of my feet as I do. My white t-shirt is balled up, half beneath the crumpled sheets of the bed, I thread it over my head, re-tie the red ribbon in my hair, finger comb through my blonde curls.

Everything takes too long, I'm too slow, sluggish, everything just being done because it's a necessity. My ears buzz, evidence of what I did seeping out between my sore thighs, cum soaking into my jeans. I wince, pursing my lips, tugging the long sleeves of my shirt over my hands. I move to the window, my heart thudding slowly in my chest, peering out, a trickle of pale moonlight revealing nothing more than a smouldering pile of ash. I sigh, my insides twisting, I glance down, watch fat teardrops hitting the carpet, splashing as they hit the toes of my boots. I close my eyes, draw in a slow breath, wipe my knuckles across my wet cheeks.

Unconsciously, I move across the room. Numbness stiffening my skeleton, my body feeling heavy, my skin too tight, my brain too loud, despite my ears unhearing, a low buzzing replacing sound. I pull open the door, the hall still in darkness, I step out, trying the other doors on my way back towards the stairs, stopping and entering when I find the bathroom.

Yellow tiles, a dark floor, no bulb in the ceiling fixture. I pee, cleaning myself up as much as I can and wash my hands, avoiding catching sight of myself in the mirrored cabinet above the sink. There's no towel, so I swipe my wet hands down my thighs, rough denim on my cold skin. Damp fingers curling over the rim of the basin, head dropping between my hunched shoulders, I breathe out, trying to exhale the knot of pain caught tangled in my chest.

Fingers itching to find a blade, carve myself free of the darkness coiling around my heart, squeezing my lungs, crushing my spine.

The mirrored cabinet above me doesn't contain much as my hand slaps against the glass, hiding my reflection from view and fumbling to tear open the door. Things fall from their shelves as I fumble, knocking things into the sink, little foil packets of half empty painkillers, cotton balls, a condom, something I didn't use. Pressing up onto tiptoes, my fingers slide over the top shelf, empty as far as I can tell.

Sighing, breath leaving me slowly, lungs deflating, I squeeze my eyes shut, shaking my head at how fucking stupid I am. I should have known, well, I don't know, I should have just fucking thought for a minute, not been so fucking *easy*. Disgust roils in my stomach, acid burning like a bolt of lightning up my throat. As if I didn't hate myself enough already, now I've got this to add to the top of the list of reasons why I do.

A glass tumbler sits on the edge of the sink, smeared and chipped, probably held toothbrushes at some point in its life, but now it's just empty, a bit like me. Reaching out, my fingers curling around the crystal glass, I turn it over in my hand, thumb rolling the base of it around in my palm. I squeeze it tightly, skin blanching white in the dark room, tips of my fingers clicking under the force. Glass rains down, the tumbler shattering into tiny shards as I launch it at the wall above the bath.

A terse scream, muffled between gritted teeth, leaves my lungs, my chest heaving. I swipe a hand over my head, fisting tight curls at the crown of my skull, yanking on the strands, fire races over my scalp, tingling in the top of my spine. Breaths come fast and hot through my nose, nostrils flaring, anger, at myself, rips through me like a blaze, an inferno scorching my core.

My nails claw at my hands, scratching, digging, gouging at the skin. I scratch at my wrists, sink down to the floor, rest my back against the wall. Thunk my head back against the cracked tiles, stare lifelessly up at the empty light fixture, I pick at my fingers, thumbs, the webbing between them, until I draw blood. I pinch the broken skin, smear sticky red across my pale skin, feel it sting and burn and soothe. Not enough.

My eyes ping open, an idea forming inside my head. Ears buzzing like flies feasting on rotten flesh inside my eardrums, I can only feel my erratic heart, strangled breathing, my uncontrolled emotion. Everything tumbling around inside of me. I know no one can get to me in here, up here. The staircase rotten. The only entrance to this floor is a death trap. One I'll have to navigate down to get the fuck out of here.

Moving to my hands and knees, crawling my heavy body across the bathroom floor, fingers curling over the edge of the bathtub, I heft myself up to my knees. Lean in, hand stretching into the tub, I finger the different shards of glass, some sharper, more jagged than others. I concentrate on their shapes and sizes, thickness, it eases my breathing, thinking about something else. Knowing what's coming. Some short, too blunt, almost rounded in their chunky edges. I find a splintered piece, it slides from the base of the avocado coloured bath, pinched between my thumb and finger, I hold it in the palm of my hand.

Waiting.

For something.

Whatever it is I think I need, in this moment, nothing could compare to what I feel when a blade pierces my skin, a slow, steady beading of blood bubbling to the surface of the slice. I take a deep breath, a shudder rocking through me. I drop my body to my haunches, twisting on the dark ground. Legs feeling like lead weights as I pull them out from under me, booted feet thunking to the floor, my legs laid out in a V before me, back against the bath. I finger the glass in my hand, running my thumb over the sharp edge, splintering and snagging at my already bleeding skin.

On instinct, muscle memory, that cathartic place I fall into each time, my fingers flick open my jeans, pushing them lower down my hips. Knowing I'll feel better after. Just one cut. One feeling. One moment. All for release. Something inside my head aches, like I've hit it, even though I haven't. I haven't touched drugs, no drink. A single sip. I shouldn't drink. Not supposed to. I think of the scar on my belly, raised and thick, curved. The supposed saving grace? It's surgically carved.

Tears drop from my lower lashes as I lift my bum, wriggle my jeans down mid-thigh, my bare arse on the cold floor sends a shiver through me when I think about where my knickers are. A fire licks through my veins as I flip my tight t-shirt up and over my belly. Fingers of my free hand find my hip bone, gliding over smooth, sliced skin, scars upon scars stacked in neat little lines over both sides. I slide my hand down lower, the inside of my thigh, much the same way but nothing as methodical. Jagged, angry scars litter the flesh there. It's proof of release versus emotions.

Glass angled between my thumb and finger, I move to my thigh, twist my leg out just slightly, knee bent, flat to the floor. Sharp point pressing on my cool skin, other hand splayed beside my hip. I suck in a deep breath, hold it in my lungs and apply pressure. The rough glass grazes through my flesh, twinkling in the small amount of light I'm gifted from the small window, as dense clouds roll across the moon.

Skin puncturing, parting, darkness beading as I glide the glass down my flesh. A second and then a third time, the fourth is harder, too much stress behind it, the glass slips from my slick fingers, my grip tight enough to make my hand bleed. I let the glass fall to the floor between my legs, the buzzing in my ears dying off.

Bloodied hand open on my other thigh, palm to ceiling, fingers loosely curled in. I lift my other from the floor, splay it over my bleeding skin, run my fingers around the wounds, over them, through them, nails plucking the slices. Gaze enchanted by the movement of my hands, I sigh calmly, hearing slowly coming back when I realise I can't hear the music anymore.

My entire body stiffens then, fear thrumming through me. Eyes adjusted to the dark, I look up, peering at the back of the closed door. Unlocked because I couldn't be bothered to fumble around in the dark long enough to look for one. I stare at it hard enough to set it on fire, willing my eyes to see through the thick wood, out into the dark hall.

Where is Blaze?

Suddenly, I feel panic like nails scratching up

my throat, claws digging and gouging at the back of my tongue. It's as though I've only now just realised the extent of the situation I find myself in. A dizzying drop back into reality, a brick of anxiety hits the pit of my stomach, and I lurch up, tearing at my jeans, slick fingers fumbling over the button and zipper. I bend low, retrieve and fist my piece of glass, not bothering to wash up first. A desperate whine caught in my throat, I realise, that all I want to do is go home, because even the cold mansion I reside in is better than here.

The door handle squeaks as I twist it, slowly pulling the door open, peering through the gap into nothing but darkness, the house creaking, silence uncomfortable, I step out into the hall. Bathroom door at my back, clicking closed, I'm light on my feet, sweeping down the hall, silence so loud now it's deafening.

Blood pounds in my ears, heart thumping erratically in my chest, rib bones bowing in, spine stiff, eyes wide, I turn at the top of the staircase. Glass in one hand, biting into my palm, blood flooding between my torn fingers, running down the length of them, dripping from my knuckles.

Free hand on the banister, I stare down into the darkness. Not a hint of life, my skin crawls like hundreds of tiny spiders are descending over my flesh. Brain foggy, I wonder, for just a second, if I've imagined it all. Sometimes I'm alone for such long periods of time, I start to question what's real and what's not.

How would I have gotten here? I don't even drive.

Squaring my shoulders, I swallow, fingers flexing over the newel post, I take a tentative step onto the first stair. One foot slightly raised off the ground, I place it down beside the first. Desperately trying to remember the path we took up here, I didn't really pay attention, I just followed where Blaze put his feet. Not even thinking about how I'd get down *without* him.

Pain bites into me like phantom teeth, I lick over my top lip, a shadow rushing past the bottom of the stairs, eyes snapping up, I freeze. Gaze boring into the pitch darkness of what's below, heart hammering away violently, beating against my breastbone, I pull in a tiny breath, just enough air to stop my lungs from screaming.

I am *petrified*.

And I think, just maybe, there's a certain thread of thrill to the fear that I *like*.

Shaking it off, I take the next step, feet angled

and pace slow, I descend into the darkness. Shadows wrap around me like a blanket of ice, the air much, much cooler than earlier, I don't know the time, I have no torch, no phone.

Della left me here.

It suddenly dawns on me then, she abandoned me as soon as we got here, she was never going to drive me home. And my stuff's in her car, a car that is likely long gone by now. It's at that chilling realisation that my boot goes through a step. Grip on the banister intense, I cling to it for dear life, pulling and shaking my foot free of the rotten wood, and just decide to risk the last five steps I have left to go. Practically throwing myself down them, the wood screeching and groaning under foot, I jump the last two, hitting the ground floor living room with a thud.

Rising from the crouch I landed in, chest heaving, my eyes fly over the dark space. Seeming so much larger than it did earlier, now empty as opposed to being full of partiers. I shiver, feeling like I'm not alone, peering around the pitch room, I eye the front door. Fist clenching around my shard of glass, I take a step towards the front door, wondering what it is I'm even going to do. I've just been left here.

Blaze forgot about me.

What did you expect?

Shaking my head, blinking back another pathetic bubble of tears, I blink hard and start heading towards the general direction of the door when heavy footfalls race down the stairs behind me. I spin in place, free hand flying to my chest, heart attacking my palm as a huge dark figure flies towards me. I back up automatically, still watching the shadowed mass descend. Hand with the glass fumbling for the door handle as my back hits wood.

The figure on the stairs, miraculously not going through any of them like I did, stops at the foot of the steps, dressed in all black, a balaclava mask covering their face, eye holes and a mouth hole, but I can't make out any of their features.

"Blaze?" I whisper his name like a prayer and a curse all rolled into one, a tiny thread of hope that's set on fire and turned to ash just as quickly as it appeared.

A dark chuckle breaks the silence, like a hot knife through butter, it's eerie and it's *not* coming from the figure a mere ten feet from me. My head snaps in the direction of the kitchen, the wide open archway now containing a second figure. Moon at their back from the kitchen window, their shadow twisting and lengthening across the already dark room.

"Blaze isn't coming, Sugar."

I tremble at the unfamiliar male voice, fingers clawing at the door, the figure at the base of the stairs unmoving, just this huge, silent, imposing shadow. My eyes flicker between the two bodies in the room with me. Lungs seizing as I breathe hard, panic like a fire burning and growing inside my chest. The second arrival takes a solid step into the room, his body even taller than the first, a bandana tied across the bridge of his nose, shaggy dark hair showing.

This all feels too familiar, too much, too *loud*. My skin itching and burning, my fingers finally latch onto the door handle, I wrench it open. Forcing me closer to the two masked strangers as it opens inwards, hitting me in the spine. Neither of them moving. I'm turning on my heels, rushing out onto the porch, the freezing wind lashing my hair across my face like a slap to my skin. I tighten my hold on the glass shard, something that soothed me now turning into a weapon. I race forward, head whipping over my shoulder, I see the two of them follow me out, a leisurely pace, arms relaxed at their sides.

I twist back to face forward, smacking into a body built like a brick wall, my nose crushed in the process. Huge hands grip my upper arms and I'm thrashing against their hold, tasting blood on my tongue, a bubble of blood gurgling at the back of my throat.

This can't be happening to me again.

I screech like a banshee, bright amber eyes peering at me through holes in a black balaclava. Hands releasing me roughly, shoving me away. I stumble, my nose gushing, hand bleeding, I dart left, sprint forward, rushing into the crops, hearing a whoop and holler at my back, footfalls chasing after me.

Ignoring it all, my breaths rasping, feet thudding, harvest leaves attacking me as I disturb them. I pant hard, desperate to put as much distance between me and those cloaked shadows as possible. No destination in mind, my real life not preparing me for this in any way, shape or form. A cry wrenches it way up my throat, I strangle it in place, trying to keep myself as quiet as possible.

I should have trained for this, prepared, done something proactive to protect myself from being the prey, again. Fear floods me, adrenaline feeding me instructions for survival, my muscles burn, skin scalding, I push myself to keep running.

Something wars inside of me, the fear choking me as much with ice as it is with fire. My lower belly churns, heat like a lick of excitement flushing through my insides, heat between my thighs, even as tears prick my eyes.

God, you're fucked up.

I smell smoke, something putrid, but I steer myself in that direction anyway, maybe there's still someone left here somewhere that has a phone. Wind rustling the crops around me, swaying them like a gently breaking wave. I break through into a clearing, heat from a bonfire hits me, the flames dying but still bright. I blink hard, eyes adjusting to the sudden intrusion of light, there's no one else here. I gag at the smell of the fire, something toxic and acrid carrying in the thick smoke.

Decaying pumpkins sat around, my eyes roving rapidly over the cleared space, a dead end to what must have been the Halloween maze. My eyes burn, tears wetting my cheeks, my feet take me back, away from the fire, towards the darkness of the throughway, I'm lost, but I can see, if I leave this clearing I'll be blind again.

Panic is a scalpel cutting into my flesh, carving

its way through skin and muscle with precision, my teeth chatter, my bones aching as I think about what to do. I hold my breath to listen, the harsh wind battering the surrounding crops, makes it impossible to hear anything over the swooshing of the harvest.

Dizziness has me reaching out, fingers trying to find something to grasp on to, I fall forward, dropping to my knees, black spots dancing across my vision. I breathe through my mouth, blood heavy and thick on my dry tongue, a shooting arrow of pain pulsing in my nose, up and into my forehead. I rock myself in the wind, my head clouding and clearing, but remaining fuzzy as I sink and lift, flitting through semi-consciousness.

Warm breath ghosts down my neck, heat engulfing my back, my eyes open lazily, like my body's already given up, *given in.*

"How good of you to wait for me," he rasps, his deep voice calm and sure. "And on your knees, pretty girl," he growls in approval.

Blaze's fingertip traces down the ridges of my spine and I shiver at his warm touch. His soft lips brush my earlobe, big body arching over me, surrounding me in a cloud of sweet caramel smoke.

"You look so pretty dressed in red." I swallow, knowing what he's referring to, blood soaking through my dark jeans, hand squeezing around glass. "Did I make you do this to yourself, pretty girl?" he asks with a smile, I feel his plush lips curl against my cheek, puckering into a feather light kiss. "Tell me." It's snapped, the order like a whip of pain striking over the backs of my thighs.

I don't lie. I nod in silence, eyes open wide, watching the three masked figures stepping into the clearing. Far enough away that they can't hear Blaze's words. Bonfire at my side, Blaze at my back, I turn my head just slightly, trying to get a look at him over my shoulder. Our lips brush, but neither one of us moves. I glance up at him, blood smeared across my face, the dripping slowed from my nose. I must look like a murder victim, but he looks at me with such fire in his gaze that I can practically see blue flames igniting in his dark eyes.

His arm sweeps forward, his large hand curling around mine, he squeezes tighter, crushing my fingers. Blood oozing painfully out of my palm, the glass digging in so hard it feels like I'll never be able to remove it.

"You like the hurt," a statement, one I neither agree or disagree with, he'll think whatever he likes either way. "You know what I think, pretty girl," it's not really a question, my eyes so drawn to his I couldn't look away if he plucked my eyeballs free from their sockets. "I think you like to be scared."

He licks his lips, eyes hungry, mouth passing over mine. His head tilts, lips slanted, he licks over my top lip with the flat of his tongue. Groaning as he tastes copper, swallowing hard, he bites down on my bottom lip, teeth scoring my swollen flesh, parted so I can breathe through my mouth, nose aching. I don't move, letting him take whatever it is he wants from me, I don't react because he's already had everything else.

"You look like you've given up," he says next, my eyes drifting closed, his words soft like a lullaby, his fingers flex around my curled fist, the point of the glass nicking his skin too.

Uncurling our joint fists after tightening so hard I see stars, he snatches the glass, flings it away from us. I breathe out a shuddery breath, fully resigning myself to whatever it is that's going to happen here tonight. His warmth shifts at my back, him on his knees, me on my haunches. He holds my cut palm up, his other hand smearing through it, I can still feel little splinters of glass in my skin when he presses hard, a hiss through my teeth.

"Do you want to make me happy, pretty girl?"

Hesitation rolls through me, the carnal need to

scream yes, the sensible part of my brain bellowing no. Why would I do anything this man wanted?

"You know you want to say yes," he purrs, the rumbling from his chest making my own ache, I feel myself lean into him, shoulder to chest where he curls around me. "I want you to come with me. Let me keep you."

Fear rocks my core, unsure what that means, heat and ice scrabbling for purchase inside me, fighting each other. One of the shadowed strangers steps forward, the shortest of the three, his wide stature imposing, shadowing me, he reaches down, large, leather gloved hand placed before me in offering. Eyes roving back to Blaze, he nods, his lips curved, his face illuminated by the fire at my side. Gaze locked on his, I reach up blindly, my hand finding warmed leather, thick fingers tighten around my own, hefting my up to my feet.

Knees wobbling and jelly-like, I peer up into warm amber orbs, thick dark lips, the rest of him covered with a black knitted mask. He spins me in his hold, my brain rushing around like liquid inside my skull. We face the fire, thick muscular arms banding around my chest, crossed over one another, squeezing my back tight to his front.

"Tell me what you see," this voice is like silk,

deep and smooth, a ghost communicating through the veil.

Trembling, eyes drawing up to the fire, I stare into it for a long time, fire, ash, embers sputtering into the air around us like tiny fireworks. Wood, and debris, all of it burning so hot, I almost don't see them. Almost.

I knock backwards, unable to get away, I thrash in the ghost's hold, nothing spiritual about it. Three bodies, or rather, what's left of them are positioned in the flames.

The smell.

I gag then, remembering the scent I followed. Bile rushes up the back of my throat, my body trembling and fighting, I claw over leather gloved hands, smearing blood everywhere I touch as I continue to bleed. Blaze steps into view, a smug little smirk on his sinfully, pretty mouth.

"Keep fighting, pretty girl."

And then a sack is going over my head, my body stiffening like rigor mortis is already setting in. Preparing me for my inevitable end. A scream dies off in my throat as a hand roughly invades the front of my jeans, fingers slipping in my arousal, sliding between my lips, harsh and not entirely unwanted.

"Oh, so you *do* like to be scared," the man from

the kitchen hums. "Fear's my favourite flavour, Sugar."

I whimper, sucking in air as the sack over my head sticks itself to my now clammy face, pulled into my mouth by my ragged breaths and he tears his hand out of my jeans like I burned him. Then I'm hauled up, thrown over a broad shoulder, my painful nose hitting into the man's rock hard arse cheek as he starts to walk.

"Careful with the merchandise," the man from the kitchen sing-song's and I feel my breath catch in my throat.

"No, no, no, no," I chant the mumble over and over, my eyes squeezed shut, not that I'd be able to see anyway. "Please, please," it's a wail, a desperate, animal cry. "Blaze, *please*."

A laugh, like a cackle makes it to my ears, like a slap to the face, a big hand smooths over my arse cheeks, and I stop breathing all together.

Memories flash through me, a sack over my head, a needle to the neck, the boot of a car. Then I wake up missing an organ and having no idea what the fuck happened.

"Please, please, no drugs, I'll be good," I cry then, tears running the wrong way up my face as I sob, rocking back and forth over the man's shoulder.

"Please, just don't drug me, please, whatever you want, please."

Nobody speaks, but I know the other men are surrounding us as we move in silence, nothing but my sobs and erratic breaths can be heard over the whip of cold wind. My occasional begging, all of it being ignored, or consumed, but no responses are given. We move for what feels like ever, footfalls thumping over dewy grounds. Slowing to a stop, I take in a deep breath, praying for something, anything, to anyone when I hear the beep of a car being unlocked and a sob rips its way up my throat.

"Please, please, don't put me in the boot, please, I'm begging you, I'll do whatever you want. I won't look, I'll be quiet, I'll be good, I won't run. *Please*." My cries are hysterical, sobbing, tears, saliva and blood alike all mixing, climbing up my face, into my hair where I hang helplessly upside down.

"*Shhh*, calm down, it's okay," Blaze says, his strong hand stroking up my spine.

I feel calmer for a second, like he's going to listen, let me inside the car like a passenger and not in the boot like a prisoner.

But then a chill rips through me as he says quietly, charming in tone.

"In the trunk, Cole. Let's go home."

And then I'm tossed in the car boot, the lid slamming down and locking me inside the darkness.

THE ASHES BOYS ARE COMING IN A FULL LENGTH NOVEL...

2023

Afterword

Okay, soooo, this was fun!

This was another 'Heron Mill Moment', that's what my friends call it when I tell them I'm going to write a book in a week and then actually do it!

But, seriously, I had fun writing this, and I can't wait to give these men more free rein in their full length novel next year!

Thank you so much for reading, I appreciate each and every one of you.

ACKNOWLEDGMENTS

Addie and Jade, for believing I could write this in a week and cheering me on the entire time. I love you like no other.

Leah, for covering this bitch and being fucking amazing. You rock and I love you, twin flame.

Inga, you last minute little gem! Thank you for everything. For your hilarious commentary through all of this. You're amazing, and I love you.

Mark, you're last but not least, because you have let me sit on my computer for the last six months without complaint. I love you so much.

ALSO BY K.L.TAYLOR-LANE

SWALLOWS AND PSYCHOS

KYLA-ROSE SWALLOW

A Dark Mafia Why Choose Romance

PURGATORY

PENANCE

PERSECUTION

CHARLIE SWALLOW

A Dark Mafia MMF Romance

RUIN

THE BLACKWELL BROTHERS

An Interconnected Series of Standalones

HUNTER BLACKWELL

A Dark Gothic Horror-esque Stepsibling MF Romance

HERON MILL

HERON MILL TENEBRIS

THORNE BLACKWELL

A Dark Gothic Mafia MF Romance

ROOK POINT

WOLF BLACKWELL

A Dark Gothic MF Romance

CARDINAL HOUSE

(COMING 2023)

THE ASHES BOYS

A Dark Bully Gang Why Choose Romance

TORMENT ME

A Bonfire Night Novella

BURY ME

A Full Length Novel

COMING 2023

FIND K.L. TAYLOR-LANE

AMAZON - K. L. Taylor-Lane

BOOKBUB - K. L. Taylor-Lane

INSTAGRAM - @kltaylorlane_author

FACEBOOK - K. L. Taylor-Lane Author

FACEBOOK READER GROUP - K's Southbrook
Psychos

GOODREADS - K. L. Taylor-Lane

PINTEREST - @KLTaylorLane

TIKTOK - @kltaylorlane.author

www.ingramcontent.com/pod-product-compliance
Lightning Source LLC
Chambersburg PA
CBHW071526170626
46811CB00007B/2961